A date with danger . . .

Suddenly a black Cadillac sedan shot out of an alley to the right of Jessica Wakefield's Jeep, narrowly missing her and Nick Fox as it turned left in front of them

"You maniac!" Jessica yelled at the other driver, but she couldn't see anyone clearly through the Cadillac's dark-tinted windows.

"Did you see . . ." she turned indignantly to Nick, only to find him slumped so far down in his seat that he was practically sitting on the floorboards. "What are you doing?" Jessica demanded, insulted. "That wasn't my fault, you know. That other car . . ."

"Shhh!" Nick interrupted, holding up one hand. "Are they following us?"

"*Following* us!" Jessica exclaimed. "Why would they . . ." Her sentence trailed off as she checked her rearview mirror. Somehow the sedan had managed to make a U-turn in the middle of the street and now it was right behind them. "Uh, yeah," she said, feeling her stomach suddenly go tense. "I think they are."

"Oh, no," Nick groaned. "They saw me."

"Who saw you?" Jessica demanded. "And why are they following you?"

"It's some guys I knew in L.A." Nick tried to peek through the back of the Jeep without being seen himself. "You're going to have to lose them."

"Lose them?" Jessica laughed. "What for?"

"They kind of want to . . . kill me."

Bantam Books in the Sweet Valley University series
Ask your bookseller for the books you have missed

#1 COLLEGE GIRLS
#2 LOVE, LIES, AND JESSICA WAKEFIELD
#3 WHAT YOUR PARENTS DON'T KNOW . . .
#4 ANYTHING FOR LOVE
#5 A MARRIED WOMAN
#6 THE LOVE OF HER LIFE
#7 GOOD-BYE TO LOVE
#8 HOME FOR CHRISTMAS
#9 SORORITY SCANDAL
#10 NO MEANS NO
#11 TAKE BACK THE NIGHT
#12 COLLEGE CRUISE
#13 SS HEARTBREAK
#14 SHIPBOARD WEDDING
#15 BEHIND CLOSED DOORS
#16 THE OTHER WOMAN
#17 DEADLY ATTRACTION
#18 BILLIE'S SECRET
#19 BROKEN PROMISES, SHATTERED DREAMS
#20 HERE COMES THE BRIDE
#21 FOR THE LOVE OF RYAN
#22 ELIZABETH'S SUMMER LOVE
#23 SWEET KISS OF SUMMER
#24 HIS SECRET PAST
#25 BUSTED!

And don't miss these Sweet Valley University Thriller Editions:

#1 WANTED FOR MURDER
#2 HE'S WATCHING YOU
#3 KISS OF THE VAMPIRE
#4 THE HOUSE OF DEATH
#5 RUNNING FOR HER LIFE
#6 THE ROOMMATE

SWEET VALLEY UNIVERSITY®

Busted!

Written by
Laurie John

Created by
FRANCINE PASCAL

BANTAM BOOKS
NEW YORK • TORONTO • LONDON • SYDNEY • AUCKLAND

RL 6, age 12 and up

BUSTED!

A Bantam Book / November 1996

Sweet Valley High® and Sweet Valley University®
are registered trademarks of Francine Pascal.
Conceived by Francine Pascal.
Produced by Daniel Weiss Associates, Inc.
33 West 17th Street
New York, NY 10011.

ISBN: 0-553-57006-4

Published simultaneously in the United States and Canada

Bantam Books are published by Bantam Books, a division of Bantam Doubleday Dell Publishing Group, Inc. Its trademark, consisting of the words "Bantam Books" and the portrayal of a rooster, is Registered in U.S. Patent and Trademark Office and in other countries. Marca Registrada. Bantam Books, 1540 Broadway, New York, New York 10036.

PRINTED IN THE UNITED STATES OF AMERICA

OPM 0 9 8 7 6 5 4 3 2 1

To Traci Ann Heller

Chapter One

Just think, Jessica Wakefield congratulated herself, pulling her long charcoal gray overcoat more snugly around her tight black turtleneck. She could feel the adrenaline pounding through her body as she hurried across the dark, deserted quad to meet Nick Fox's mystery caller. *If I hadn't answered Nick's phone, I'd be missing all this!*

Not that she was exactly sure what "all this" was. The only thing Jessica could gather from the cellular phone call she'd intercepted Saturday evening, at Tom Watts's surprise birthday party, was that her mysterious boyfriend, Nick, was supposed to meet someone for a secret pickup behind the science building fifteen minutes ago. But Nick wasn't going to show up—Jessica was.

Jessica checked her watch distractedly as she

left the quad. It was two-fifteen Sunday morning. She ran down the walkway toward the meeting place, the hem of her coat flapping loosely about the calves of her black leggings. It had taken so long to say good night to Nick, get home, and put together the perfect "spy" outfit that she was a little behind schedule. *I look great, though.* She smiled to herself, adjusting her black felt hat.

The prospect of finding out who Nick Fox really was and what he was hiding from her was even more thrilling than running alone across the pitch-black Sweet Valley University campus. Jessica was sure Nick was some kind of secret government agent. FBI, maybe, or even CIA. It was pretty clear that Nick *wanted* to tell her everything about himself, but for some reason he couldn't.

Whatever he's doing, he probably thinks it's too dangerous for me to know about, Jessica guessed as the science building finally came into view. *But I'll show him what Jessica Wakefield is made of!* She turned the last corner and rounded the end of the looming rectangular building, her heart beating wildly. Behind the science building the darkness was so complete that Jessica could barely see.

"Hello?" she whispered breathlessly, pausing to listen. "Is anybody there?"

No one answered. As exciting as the whole situation was, it was undeniably creepy behind the deserted building, and Jessica shivered as she made her way slowly along a narrow gravel path through the overgrown landscaping.

"Hello?" she tried again. The blood in her ears was pounding so loudly, she wasn't even sure she'd be able to hear if someone answered her.

"D'ya got it?" rasped a deep, sudden voice at her back.

Jessica whirled, startled, to see a shadowy shape lurking in the tall bushes at the side of the path.

"Of course," she managed, struggling to regain her composure. *Got what?* she wondered.

"Hand it over, then," Nick's mystery appointment grunted. The shadow was a man—a big man—but that was all Jessica could tell in the near-total blackness.

"Not so fast," she improvised. "Don't you have something for me too?"

"No kidding," the man returned sarcastically.

Jessica couldn't help being a little surprised—she had expected a secret agent to be more sophisticated. Still, maybe this guy wasn't an agent—maybe he was just some sort of contact. Perhaps he had information Nick wanted. Government secrets, even! Jessica felt another thrill course through her at the thought of being involved in something so glamorous and dangerous.

"Well, give it to me, then," she directed

vaguely, hoping she sounded as though she knew what she was doing.

The man in the bushes didn't say anything for a moment, then he took a menacing half step forward. "Who are you anyway?" he demanded, his voice hard and frightening. "Where's Nick?"

"Nick sent me to cover for him," Jessica answered nervously.

"To cover *what?*" the voice rasped sharply.

"You know," Jessica fumbled. "The, uh . . . pickup."

The man hesitated for a second, then retreated back into the bushes. "If you're here for the pickup, you'd better show me some cash. Now."

Uh-oh, Jessica thought, feeling her empty pockets. Why hadn't it occurred to her before that this guy might want to be paid? What was she going to do?

"First tell me what you have for me," she directed hopefully. If she wasn't going to be able to buy the "pickup," she could at least find out what it was.

"You've got to be kidding," Nick's contact spat, furious. "What do you think this is? D'ya got the money or not?"

"Well, not *here* . . . ," Jessica began, hoping to stall him, but the man was already running away, crashing through the bushes and swearing violently.

"Wow," Jessica whispered to herself as his broad, angry back was absorbed into the night. Then she pulled her black hat down lower over her face and hustled in the other direction. Nick was running with some pretty scary characters.

Jessica felt safer when she'd rounded the end of the science building again and begun crossing the empty pavement in front of it. At least there were a few tiny security lights there, so she could be sure she was alone. If only she'd brought some money! Not that she would have had enough, but if she'd emptied her savings, she could have flashed a couple of hundred-dollar bills around. Would that have kept Nick's contact interested?

"I wonder what government secrets sell for these days," Jessica said aloud as she regained the edge of the quad and sank down on a bench to rest.

Now that the excitement of her secret meeting was wearing off, Jessica felt totally let down. Tonight had seemed like such a good opportunity to finally learn something about her new boyfriend, Nick—something *other* than the fact that he was the sexiest man alive. But Jessica's hopes had been completely destroyed. She hadn't learned a thing.

Sighing, Jessica checked her watch again. Between Tom's party and the mystery meeting, it had been a long night, and now it was 2:35 on

Sunday morning. "What a total waste of time," she grumbled, rising and starting for home. "And I don't even get to sleep in tomorrow."

Elizabeth Wakefield hummed happily, eating a bagel, as she bustled around the dorm room she shared with her twin, Jessica. The unexpectedly warm fall sunshine that streamed through the windows created patterns on the floor. Normally Elizabeth would have eaten in the cafeteria, but today she was too tired to make her way over there. Her surprise party for Tom's twenty-first birthday the night before had been a total success, and Elizabeth's present to Tom had been the biggest surprise of all—a father and a family of his own.

Ever since Tom's entire family had been killed in a car crash, Tom had been in extended mourning. Not only did he miss them horribly; he blamed himself for the accident. Elizabeth knew it had never occurred to Tom that the man who had died that day wasn't his natural father. It had never occurred to her either—until she'd met George Conroy. What were the odds that this total stranger looking for his long-lost son would turn out to be Tom's father? Elizabeth could barely keep from laughing with joy as she mentally replayed her role in bringing the two men together.

"Save a bite for me," a groggy voice said, interrupting Elizabeth's thoughts.

"Jessica!" Elizabeth exclaimed, shocked. "What are *you* doing up so early?"

"Hating life," replied her twin sister as she pushed her tousled blond hair out of her blue-green eyes. Jessica put on loose jeans and a half buttoned flannel shirt, but she still looked half asleep. "Why do people get up at this painful hour?" she asked grouchily.

"More important," Elizabeth countered, wiping her hands on a napkin to keep her own perfectly pressed white sundress neat. "Why are *you* up this early? You're scaring me, Jess."

"Very funny," Jessica retorted. "You don't have any of those coffee bag things, do you?"

"Actually, yeah. Do you want one?"

"Please." It sounded more like a groan than a request.

Elizabeth couldn't help smiling as she added more hot water to the electric kettle, then took another bite of her bagel. By the time she had finished the first half, the kettle was whistling, and Elizabeth poured the boiling water into two communal coffee mugs.

"Here," Elizabeth said, putting Jessica's mug on the desk and tossing a foil-wrapped coffee bag down beside it. "You look like death warmed over, by the way. What time did you go to bed?"

This time Jessica really did groan. "Don't ask."

"I saw you leave the party," Elizabeth remembered. "But I never heard you come in last night."

Jessica didn't respond.

"Hey, you didn't really want a bite, did you?" Elizabeth asked suddenly. "I'll share my last half."

"I was kidding," Jessica said, looking as if the very thought of a waffle made her sick. "Anyway, I'm meeting Nick for breakfast." She pulled the foil off her coffee bag and dunked it under the steaming water.

"Ah." Elizabeth smiled. "That explains it. I knew you weren't up this early just to shoot the breeze with your sister—no matter how gifted a conversationalist she is."

"You're in a good mood," Jessica observed darkly. She dunked the bag in and out of the water repeatedly in an effort to make her coffee as black as possible.

"You're right," Elizabeth agreed. "Didn't you think the party last night was fabulous? Tom was so surprised."

"Who wouldn't have been?" Jessica asked. "I mean, finding out you have a father, a brother, *and* a sister after you've spent the last few years thinking you were alone in the world must be pretty weird. You're lucky he didn't freak out on you."

"I knew he wouldn't," Elizabeth said, pausing thoughtfully with a bite of bagel halfway to her mouth. "Sometimes I think that having a family is the most important thing in the world to Tom." She resumed eating. "Anyway, it was a little awkward at first, but you could tell that he and Mr. Conroy were both incredibly happy. And after half an hour it was like they'd known each other all their lives."

Jessica took Elizabeth's spoon and pinned the exhausted coffee bag to the bottom of her cup, trying to squeeze out any last juice before she finally fished it out and laid it on a napkin. "So what are they doing this morning?" she asked.

"I think they're meeting for breakfast somewhere," Elizabeth said, "and then they're spending the whole day together. I'll catch up with them tonight before Mr. Conroy goes back to Los Angeles. Oh, Jess," Elizabeth added with a happy sigh, "I'm just so happy that Tom has a family again and that I was able to help make it happen."

Jessica looked up from her coffee mug, which she was gripping with both hands. "It's nice," she agreed, so obviously sincere that Elizabeth could feel herself glowing all over.

Jessica didn't always see Elizabeth's point of view, of course. In fact, there had probably never been two identical twins with more different personalities. Although the sisters shared long blond hair, aquamarine eyes, and perfect five-foot, six-inch figures, Jessica had a wild streak that was notorious for getting her in trouble, whereas Elizabeth was cautious, thoughtful, and studious.

The twins had always been close in spite of their differences, however, and it meant a lot to Elizabeth that Jessica approved of what she'd done for Tom.

"Thanks," Elizabeth said happily, finishing off the last of her breakfast with relish. "It *is* nice."

Jessica was halfway through her coffee and starting to look a little more alive, Elizabeth noticed. "So what are you and Nick doing today?" Elizabeth asked. "I mean, after breakfast."

"Nick has to study, I think, so I'll probably go over to Theta house."

"Oh, definitely," Elizabeth teased. "No point in studying yourself."

Jessica raised a warning eyebrow, but Elizabeth just laughed. Nothing could spoil her mood today. She couldn't even remember the last time everything in her life had been so absolutely perfect.

After a moment Jessica grinned as well. "I can't believe I'm up at six-thirty just to meet a guy for breakfast," she admitted. "The things I'll do for love!"

"*I* can't believe that's what you're going to wear," Elizabeth said, eyeing her sister's sloppy outfit. "And anyway, it's after seven now."

"Seven!" Jessica gasped, whipping around to check the clock on the wall behind her. "I still have to shower and change and . . ." The rest of the sentence was lost as Jessica ran from the room in a panic.

"I hope no one gets between her and the bathroom." Elizabeth laughed to herself as Jessica disappeared down the hallway. "Or somebody's going to get hurt!"

This isn't exactly what I had in mind, Alexandra Rollins thought with annoyance as she stuffed another envelope. When Nick Fox had suggested she call the SVU Drug and Alcohol Abuse Hot Line the night before, it had seemed like such a good idea that Alex had impulsively decided to volunteer there instead. After all, she was no stranger to hot lines, and Alex had thought that talking to other people with alcohol addictions might keep her from wanting to take a drink herself. The problem was, though, she wasn't talking to anybody—she was stuck in a hard folding chair stuffing stupid flyers into envelopes. She wished she'd never walked through their doors.

She wished she'd never done a lot of things, for that matter. The fight she'd had with her boyfriend, Noah Pearson, a couple of days before, for example—she definitely could have skipped that. It was just that sometimes Noah didn't have a clue. After all, how could he? He thought he knew everything about her drinking problem, but he'd never been through the horrible things she'd been through—the cravings, the blackouts, the destructive public losses of self-control, the long, uphill battle to regain even the smallest amount of dignity and self-respect.

Alex closed her eyes as the nasty breakup scene between her and Noah surfaced in her memory. How could he have been so cold and condescending, accusing her of wanting pity when she only needed his support? She'd read it in his face, how little he believed in her. Oh, sure, he tried to build her up when things went wrong, but it always felt more like Noah just refused to admit she could have a problem than real encouragement. She'd only told him how much she wanted a drink so that he'd understand what she was going through—she'd never intended to give in to the urge. But Noah had totally panicked. She'd seen it in his eyes, and it had made her sick at heart.

Alex opened her eyes and savagely resumed stuffing the hot line's envelopes. Noah used to know her so much better when he'd worked as an operator at the main campus hot line. In fact, Alex had more or less met him that way. Part of the reason the bond between them had been so strong back then was that they'd spent so much time talking and really getting to know each other before they'd even gone out on a date. But the last time Alex had seen Noah—at Tom Watts's birthday party—he'd had his arm around that suck-up Tiffany Harkins. *Don't think about it!* she ordered herself roughly, blinking back tears.

"So how's it going?" a friendly male voice asked unexpectedly from across the tiny room.

Startled, Alex looked up. "OK," she answered coolly, pulling herself back together.

The guy who had spoken was named Doug Chandler. He ran the substance abuse hot line, and it was Doug who had given her the exciting task of stuffing envelopes. Doug crossed the shabby room in two short steps and sat in a metal folding chair on the other side of the card table where Alex was working. He grabbed a short stack of the folded green flyers from the box and began expertly stuffing them into envelopes, finishing three for every one of Alex's.

"I really appreciate you helping us out with this mailing," Doug said, never breaking rhythm. "I know it's not the most glamorous job in the world, but believe me, it's very important."

"That's OK," Alex said.

"You see, most of our funding comes from private donations. If we didn't send out these pledge requests, we couldn't stay open." He smiled, and Alex felt her anger toward him melt. He was very good-looking, in a jeans-and-plaid-flannel, outdoorsy kind of way.

Stuffing envelopes isn't that bad, she told herself, smiling back. *As long as it's really important.*

"Sunday mornings are probably our busiest time too," Doug added, grabbing another stack of flyers. "You know, with everybody feeling bad about all the partying they did on Saturday night."

Alex remembered how very close she herself had come to "partying" the night before and shuddered. "Yeah," she said quietly. "I do know."

Doug's brown eyes were sympathetic. "That's OK," he said, briefly touching the back of her hand. "It'll be a big asset when you start working the phones. People who've been through it themselves always make the best counselors."

"Really?" Alex asked hopefully.

"Oh, absolutely," Doug said. "They have a firsthand understanding of the problem that outsiders never acquire. Uh, to put that in English, they know what they're talking about."

Alex laughed. "It's not exactly a gift."

"No," Doug agreed, returning her smile, "but you might as well use it." He took the envelopes he had stuffed and threw them into the box at Alex's side. "Well, that looks like all of them," he said.

"What?" Alex exclaimed, turning her head toward the stack of flyers yet to be stuffed. To her amazement, it was gone. "Wow," she said. "You're really fast."

Doug blew at the tip of his right index finger as if it were a smoking gun. "Fastest fingers in the West," he bragged. "Besides, I've stuffed so many envelopes for the hot line that I lost track a long time ago."

"So now what do you want me to do?" Alex asked, suddenly afraid that Doug would send her home.

"Well," he said, "of course you can leave if you want to—"

"I don't want to," Alex put in quickly.

"Or you can come on back to the phone room and listen to me take a couple of calls."

"I'd love to," Alex said. Rising from her uncomfortable folding chair, Alex smoothed her short leather skirt nervously and followed Doug through the doorway he'd come in by. She couldn't help wishing she'd dressed down a little, especially now that she'd seen how casual Doug was. A second later they were in the "phone room," and Alex finally grasped what a tiny, shoestring operation the hot line really was. The "reception" area where she'd been working was about the size of the average bathroom, and the phone room was only slightly larger. Those appeared to be the only two rooms.

"Is this it?" Alex blurted before she could stop herself.

"This is it," Doug agreed, completely unperturbed. He gestured grandly with one hand as Alex took in the three operator stations facing three corners of the tiny, windowless room. The doorway where she and Doug stood occupied the fourth corner. "What do you think?" he asked.

"It's, uh, not what I expected," Alex admitted.

"Life never is," Doug remarked, heading for the empty station. "Here, have a seat. I'd introduce you around, but Cindy and Richard are on calls."

"That's OK," Alex said, taking the folding chair Doug offered. Cindy and Richard wore operator's headsets to help them screen out distracting noises from the rest of the room. They seemed oblivious to Doug and Alex's presence as they sat listening intently, their backs to the center of the room.

"The first and foremost duty of a hot-line operator isn't to talk—it's to listen," Doug began, putting on his own headset. "Most people who call here don't call because they want us to tell them what to do. They call because they feel like there's no one else they can talk to—no one who understands."

Once again Alex remembered her fight with Noah. As much as he wanted to understand her problem, he just didn't. "I know what you mean," she told Doug.

Doug nodded. "It's really important to let the callers talk. Let them get it all out, and whatever you do, don't interrupt them. If they ask you a question, you can answer it, and if they stop talking, you can say something. But mostly you just listen. Got it?"

"Got it," Alex agreed.

"OK, I'm going to take a call now, and I'll put it on the loudspeaker so you can hear too," Doug said, reaching for a light on the switchboard. "Oh yeah," he added, pausing, "I hope this goes without saying, but anything you hear here is one hundred percent confidential. It doesn't leave this room, no matter what. Can you handle that?"

"I can handle it," Alex assured him.

"Good." Doug flipped the switch. "SVU Substance Abuse Hot Line," he said calmly into his microphone. "What can I help you with?"

At first Alex thought the loudspeaker wasn't working, but finally she heard a little sniffle.

"I don't know," said a girl's voice, thick with emotion. It was obvious the caller had been crying, probably for hours. "I feel so stupid wasting your time. It's just that . . . well, I'm only a freshman and I don't know who else to call."

Alex's heart turned over. She felt as if she knew this girl. In a way she *was* this girl.

"You're not wasting anyone's time," Doug assured the caller. "Why don't you tell me about it?"

The girl drew a shaky breath. "It's just that everything moves so fast here," she said. "Back home, where I come from, everything's a lot easier. But I really want to fit in at college, you know?"

"Yeah," Doug said. "I do."

"I never got in any kind of trouble before. I mean, not in high school. But it seems like every time I go to a party here, everyone's drinking and having fun. I feel like I'll stick out if I don't drink too. The thing is, I only do it because I want people to like me. Isn't that stupid?"

"A lot of people feel the same pressure," Doug said neutrally.

"Yeah. But last night—" The caller broke off, and Alex could hear muffled sobbing. *The poor girl,* Alex thought. She turned to Doug, begging him with her eyes to do something, but he simply held an index finger to his lips.

"Last night," the girl finally resumed. "Well . . . I don't remember much about last night." There was a long pause.

"Did you black out?" Doug asked at last.

"I guess that's it," the caller agreed. "I must have. I remember going to a fraternity party with my roommate, and everyone was drinking some kind of deadly green punch with dry ice in it. It tasted disgusting, but I didn't want to look like a lightweight, so I drank some. I remember having the first glass.

"Then this guy asked me to dance and he seemed pretty nice. I think he brought me a second glass. There might have been another one after that—I'm not sure.

"Then . . . then we went to his room, I think. We were someplace in the frat house. He was kissing me. I wanted him to stop, but I was so drunk, I couldn't push him off me. I remember thinking that stopping him was more trouble than it was worth. . . ." The caller trailed off in a fresh fit of sobs.

"Did he rape you?" Doug asked at last. Alex held her breath for the answer.

"No," the girl said. "No, I don't think so. But this morning I woke up on a bench in the quad. My blouse was ripped and my lips were bruised. I don't even remember how I got there. What should I do?"

"You have lots of different options," Doug told her. "What do you *want* to do?"

"I don't know." The caller groaned. "I guess I want to stop. I just feel so alone, you know? I mean, what if everyone thinks I'm not fun?"

"I guess you have to decide exactly what type of fun you're willing to be," Doug suggested. "For example, that frat guy probably thought you were pretty fun, but it didn't make you happy."

"No. It didn't," the girl agreed.

"There are all kinds of organizations on campus that do fun things without drugs and alcohol. Do you have a modem?"

"Sure."

"I'm going to give you a number," Doug said. "Dial into this site and you'll get a complete listing of all the clubs and groups on campus and information about joining them. Are you ready?"

"Yes," the girl answered. Doug read her the number, and Alex felt as if she could practically see the caller writing it down at the other end.

"I'm going to give you another number too," Doug said. "It's for a freshman support group. A lot of people have trouble their first year in college—it's more common than you think. This is a really good group to hang out with and make some new friends."

"Thanks," the caller said gratefully after Doug read her the second number. "You're a real lifesaver."

"No problem," Doug told her warmly. "You call back to talk anytime you want."

"That was so great!" Alex exclaimed the second Doug disconnected the line. "You really helped that girl!"

"That's what we're here for," Doug reminded her, smiling.

"I know," Alex said excitedly. "But I mean, you really *helped* her."

"Yeah, I think so," Doug agreed. "Don't be so impressed. That was an easy call."

"Easy?" Alex echoed. It had seemed like a miracle to her.

"That girl isn't a hard drinker," Doug explained. "Did you listen? She never once said that she *wanted* to drink, that she *had* to drink. She's just lonely and insecure. If she can find some friends who share her interests, I think she'll be fine."

"You're right," Alex agreed slowly. She'd been so caught up in the emotion of the call, she'd missed that simple, important point. Alex had just assumed that anyone who drank must crave alcohol the way she herself did. Then Alex realized something else. The entire time she'd been listening to the caller, she'd never once experienced a desire to drink herself—if anything, she'd been repulsed by the consequences.

"I think I'm going to like volunteering here," Alex said, smiling.

She finally knew what she had to do to get her problem under control. *You're a real lifesaver,* the girl had told Doug. Alex would be a lifesaver too.

Chapter Two

"Hey there, Sunshine," Nick called out as Jessica pulled her red Jeep up to the curb behind the student center and stopped it. "Good morning!"

"It's only eight o'clock," Jessica grumbled, peering over the tops of her dark glasses. "I'd like to know what's so good about that." Even though she was happy to see Nick, Jessica was still upset about having to get up and rush around so early on a Sunday.

Nick laughed, climbed into the passenger seat, and buckled his seat belt. "Not a morning person, I see," he observed as Jessica pulled back into traffic.

"Not remotely," she confirmed. But secretly she could feel herself starting to come around. After all, the sight of Nick wearing shorts was worth getting up for, wasn't it? Jessica checked him out from the right side of her dark glasses as she drove, taking in his tan, muscular legs, his broad chest and shoulders, and his impossibly handsome face with those killer green eyes. She was definitely glad she'd taken the time to wash her hair and change into her pink miniskirt and new lace-trimmed white camisole.

The sun beat down on them in the open Jeep while Jessica drove, making it feel like summer. The weather, Nick—all of it seemed almost too good to be true, and Jessica smiled in spite of the early hour. "So where do you want to eat?" she asked as they cleared the edge of campus.

"I have the perfect place for *you* this morning," Nick teased. "How about the Crazy Crab?"

"Is that supposed to be a joke?" Jessica asked testily, her good mood slipping a little.

"Well, sort of." Nick laughed. "But there really is such a place, and they do a great breakfast. Haven't you ever been there?"

"I've never even heard of it."

"Oh!" Nick said excitedly. "We have to go, then. It's down at the beach, and I'll warn you in advance the decor is a little hokey—you know, fake pirate style. But the food! Out of this world."

Jessica was smiling again. "There's only so much you can do with eggs and toast," she said.

Nick put on a look of mock injury. "You're wrong," he told her. "Turn left at the corner up here and I'll show you a shortcut."

Jessica turned as instructed, amused at the notion of Nick showing *her* a shortcut. After all, she'd lived in Sweet Valley all her life. Nick had just transferred to SVU from somewhere in northern California and before that he'd lived in Los Angeles.

At least, that's what he'd claimed. But if he'd really only been in Sweet Valley a few days, how did he know his way around so well, let alone know shortcuts? How come he was such an expert on restaurants Jessica had never heard of? She was just about to ask him when a black Cadillac sedan shot out of an alley to their right, narrowly missing the Jeep as it turned left in front of them.

"You maniac!" Jessica yelled irately at the other driver, but she couldn't see anyone clearly through the Cadillac's dark-tinted windows.

"Did you see . . ." She turned indignantly to Nick, only to find him slumped so far down in his seat that he was practically sitting on the floorboards. "What are you doing?" Jessica demanded, insulted. "That wasn't my fault, you know. That other car—"

"Shhh!" Nick interrupted, holding up one hand. "Are they following us?"

"*Following* us!" Jessica exclaimed. "Why would they be . . ." Her sentence trailed off as she checked her rearview mirror. Somehow the sedan had managed to make a U-turn in the middle of the street and now it was right behind them. "Uh, yeah," she said, feeling her stomach suddenly go tense. "I think they are."

"Oh no." Nick groaned. "They saw me."

"Who saw you?" Jessica asked, not quite sure if the gastrointestinal butterflies she was experiencing meant she was scared or just really excited. "And why are they following us?"

"It's some guys I knew in L.A.," Nick said, trying to peek through the back of the Jeep without being seen himself. "You're going to have to lose them."

"Lose them?" Jessica laughed. "What for?"

Nick sighed impatiently, and Jessica could tell he wasn't interested in answering questions. Still, she wasn't doing anything he said until she knew what was going on.

"They kind of want to . . . kill me," Nick admitted at last, glancing back over his shoulder again.

"*Kill* you!" Jessica exclaimed. "How come?"

"I just . . . I lived in a really bad neighborhood, OK?" Nick said urgently. "Now can you please drive? I'm not kidding."

"Wow," breathed Jessica. She had never seen such a worried look in Nick's eyes before. He was in trouble—and she was just the girl to help him! Jessica checked her rearview mirror one last time, then put the gas pedal straight to the floor. The Jeep leaped forward crazily, and Jessica immediately whipped it into a sharp right turn and rocketed down a deserted side street.

"Impressive," Nick murmured approvingly, moving partway back into his seat.

That was all the encouragement Jessica needed.

The Cadillac had managed the corner and was already gaining on her bumper as Jessica spun the steering wheel hard to the left, then hard to the left again. Streets, houses, and businesses flew by in a blur as Jessica kept the accelerator down, turning right, then left, then right again—anything to confuse the other driver.

"I think we're losing them," she yelled excitedly as the black car dropped back a little.

"You're doing fine," Nick said calmly. He was all the way back in his seat now, his eyes on the road ahead of them. "Just keep doing what you're doing."

"Right!" Jessica turned a double hard left, watching in her rearview mirror as the big black sedan fishtailed almost out of control. "They can't keep up with me!" she crowed.

"They can't turn as tight as you can," Nick corrected, "but believe me, that's a fast car. Don't let them catch you on a straightaway."

"Don't worry," Jessica bragged. "I'll take them on a tour of Sweet Valley they'll never forget!"

Jessica was giddy with excitement as she shot erratically through the streets of the beach district, keeping her runs short and her turns sharp. She knew she could lose the Cadillac—it was only a matter of time. After all, hadn't she grown up in this town? *No one knows these streets better than I do,* she congratulated herself as she made a fast right, then left, then right. *As long as I stay off Beachview Road we should . . .*

Suddenly the ocean sprang into view in front of them—the Jeep was practically on the sand! Reacting quickly, Jessica pulled the wheel into a hard right turn as the road they were racing down dead-ended into a wide highway paralleling the beach.

"Uh-oh," she breathed as they sped along the highway, the ocean on their left. Jessica's foot stomped reflexively on the gas pedal, but it was already to the floor.

"What?" Nick asked.

"Nothing," she said, checking her mirror frantically. How could she have been so *stupid?* All that turning . . . they were on Beachview!

"What?" Nick demanded.

"Uh, we're kind of in trouble," Jessica admitted, checking her mirror again. The Jeep was practically flying down the wide divided highway, but the black sedan was gaining fast.

"What *kind* of trouble?" Nick asked, watching the other car overtake them.

"It's just that . . . well, I didn't mean to take this road," Jessica yelled over the engine—it was whining, full out. "There aren't any exits for probably five miles and there's no way to turn around either."

"Five miles!" Nick exploded. "They'll catch us for sure!"

"I'm sorry," Jessica shouted back, feeling helpless. The menacing black car was still gaining steadily from behind.

"Does this Jeep have four-wheel drive?" Nick asked suddenly.

"Of course," Jessica answered. "Why?"

"On-the-fly?" he persisted.

"Yes, but—" Before Jessica could finish her question, Nick grabbed the steering wheel from her hands, pulling it to the right. The Jeep careened wildly toward the right side of the road, crossing two empty traffic lanes. Just ahead Jessica could see the wide concrete bridge spanning Cooper Canyon and the railroad tracks down below.

"Nick!" she screamed. "You're going to run us off the road!"

"That's the idea," he agreed through gritted teeth. "Hang on!"

A second later the Jeep lurched sickeningly as first the right and then the left wheels exited the pavement. For a moment Jessica was so panicked that everything went white. Then she realized they weren't hurtling through space, but rather down a steep dirt access road that workers used to maintain the bridge supports and train tracks. Shakily she put her hands back on the steering wheel, trying to help Nick control the speeding vehicle. The bottom of the hill was coming up fast, and Jessica could see the steel rails clearly now in the shade underneath the bridge.

"Put it in four-wheel drive!" Nick shouted, still wrestling with the bucking steering wheel. Jessica did as he asked just as the Jeep hit flat ground. "Left! Turn left!" Nick yelled.

Jessica grabbed control of the wheel, steering hard to the left under the bridge. The ocean sparkled in the distance ahead of her. If they went very far, she realized, they were going to end up on the beach. "Are they still following us?" Jessica asked. The Jeep was bouncing too crazily on the rutted dirt road for her to find anything in the mirrors.

"I sure hope so," Nick answered, twisting around in his seat.

"But Nick!" Jessica protested. "I'm going to run out of road!"

"Just keep going. Head straight across the sand," he instructed. "There they are. What idiots!"

"Are they coming?" Jessica asked. As she spoke, her tires lurched off the end of the packed-dirt road and spun momentarily in the soft sand of the beach. The Jeep regained traction and shot forward toward the ocean.

"Yes, they're coming," Nick said happily.

Jessica shot him a confused look. He was sitting way up and backward in his seat now, smiling broadly.

"What . . . ?" she began.

"Yes!" he bellowed suddenly, throwing his arms into the air as if his team had just scored the winning touchdown. "*Yes!* Jessica, you're brilliant!"

The Jeep was still speeding through the loose sand, but Jessica turned her head to look anyway, trying to see what had happened.

"They're stuck," Nick explained. "All the way

up to the axles. Man, are they going to be furious!"

He laughed, showing his perfect white teeth, and Jessica joined in, exhilarated. They had escaped! Not only that, but she was "brilliant." Reaching the packed wet sand at last, Jessica turned left, in the direction of town, then drove about a mile along the breakers before she stopped.

"That was outrageous!" she said, throwing herself into Nick's open arms.

"No, *you're* outrageous. Thank you," he said, just as their lips came together. They kissed next to the glittering ocean, the sun warm on their bodies, until Jessica felt as if she were floating. This guy had it all! Looks, excitement, passion.

"Are you sure we didn't die?" she murmured, her fingers buried in Nick's thick brown hair. "I think I'm in heaven."

Nick held her more tightly, protectively, and her hands traveled down his neck to his broad, sun-warmed shoulders. She could feel the taut, bunched muscles beneath the thin cotton of his T-shirt.

He's so tense, Jessica thought, only vaguely remembering that moments before their lives had been in danger.

"Jessica," Nick said at last, pushing her gently away. "We'd better get going." He glanced behind them in the direction of their luckless pursuers. "I mean, I don't think we need to worry, but I'd prefer to be back on a road—just in case."

Jessica felt the excitement of potential danger

trickle into her veins again. "Nick," she began, settling back into her seat, "why were those guys chasing you?"

He looked uncomfortable. "I told you."

"Not really," she persisted. "I don't think 'living in a bad neighborhood' is much of an answer." Her blue-green eyes narrowed with the intensity of her interest. "What's your real story?"

Nick couldn't hold her gaze. He tried for only a moment before he turned away and looked out to sea. "I can't tell you," he mumbled. "I . . ." The end of his sentence was spoken so softly that it was completely lost beneath the sound of the waves.

"What?" Jessica prompted.

"Nothing," he said, turning to look at her again. "Please, Jessica. Don't ask me anything else."

"But—"

"Jessica!"

"All right," Jessica agreed reluctantly, starting the engine again and driving slowly down the sand in the direction of town. She was still burning with curiosity, but she couldn't keep a sly smile off her face just the same. She thought she'd heard what Nick had whispered when he'd turned his head away—*I wish I could,* he'd said. Nick *wanted* to tell her what was going on, but for some unknown reason he was holding back. Well, he couldn't put her off forever.

I'll find out what he's up to if it's the last thing I ever do, Jessica promised herself silently.

* * *

"I feel thoroughly virtuous," Nina Harper announced as she followed Elizabeth down the library stairs and into the warm noon sunshine. "What do you say to some lunch?"

Elizabeth laughed. "I got a lot done too, but I don't know if I earned lunch. You didn't see the waffles I had for breakfast."

"Waffles!" Nina exclaimed in mock horror. "It's salad for you, then, I'm afraid."

"Yeah. All right," Elizabeth agreed, turning her steps in the direction of the cafeteria.

The weather outside was beautiful. Even though it was Sunday, students were lying all over the close-cropped green lawns—studying, talking, or just working on their tans. Elizabeth's spirits soared as the two friends crossed campus together, soaking in the sunshine.

"I'm so happy!" she told Nina contentedly, stretching her bare arms lazily in front of her.

"Tom's party was a major success," Nina replied, guessing the source of her friend's enthusiasm. Like Elizabeth, Nina was wearing a sundress, but hers was a bright tropical print.

"Yes," Elizabeth agreed. "But not just the party. It's great that Tom has a family of his own again too."

Nina nodded. "It obviously means a lot to him."

"Oh, it does," Elizabeth confirmed. "It's hard to believe how much. I mean, it was as if he never really felt whole before. There was always this enormous void that only a family could fill."

Nina looked surprised. "You're exaggerating."

"I'm not," Elizabeth said. "It's great to finally see him so happy. Not only that, I'm really hoping that now that Tom feels more grounded, we'll be able to move to a whole new level in our relationship."

Nina shook her head and her new hairstyle tossed with the motion, temporarily distracting Elizabeth from the subject of Tom. Nina had worn her black hair braided and beaded ever since before Elizabeth had met her, but only the day before she'd made the change to a softly curled, shoulder-brushing cut.

"I can't get over the lack of beads," Elizabeth said, smiling at her friend.

"I thought you said you liked it!" Nina cried, running a dark hand nervously over her new, beadless locks.

"I do," Elizabeth assured her. "I like it a lot. It's just . . . different."

"Different . . . how?" Nina asked suspiciously.

"I don't know," Elizabeth answered. "More sophisticated, I guess."

Nina relaxed visibly. "Well," she said, "that's all right, then."

"What's all right?" asked a friendly voice behind them. Elizabeth turned, but no one was there. A basketball slapped the pavement on her other side and Elizabeth turned that way, glimpsing Todd Wilkins just as he tried to dodge behind her again.

"Ah," he said with a laugh. "You caught me."

"Hi, Todd," Elizabeth and Nina said in unison.

Todd was looking exceptionally good, Elizabeth noticed. He was dressed for basketball, in shorts and a tank top, and the sun glinted off the sweat on his broad, muscular shoulders. He was still tan from the summer, and his wavy brown hair was full of blond highlights. His large, strong hands twirled a regulation basketball as he walked backward on the sidewalk in front of the girls.

"What are you two up to?" he asked.

"We just finished a major cram session in the library," Elizabeth explained. "And now we're going to lunch. How about you?"

Todd spun the basketball expertly on one extended finger. "Working out," he said with a laugh. "Well, sort of. I was playing pickup over by the gym."

"I guess you're pretty glad to be back on the basketball team this year," Nina observed.

Todd's eyes went round. "*Pretty* glad?" he repeated. "More like ecstatic."

He really *did* look ecstatic, Elizabeth realized. Better than he'd looked in a very long time.

"It must be weird for you with Gin-Yung gone," Elizabeth said. "Do you miss her a lot?" Todd and Gin-Young had been dating before Gin-Yung had left to spend the semester studying in

London and covering soccer for a newspaper there.

Todd looked a little sheepish. "Not really," he admitted. "I mean, we're still good friends, but the boyfriend-girlfriend thing is over. I got a letter from her yesterday, though."

"And how does she like her new school?" Nina asked.

"OK, I guess," Todd answered. A brief flicker of doubt crossed his face. "To tell the truth, I'm a little worried about that. Every time she writes, Gin-Yung tells me how tired she is—like maybe she's depressed or something. I mean, that's not normal, is it?"

"It's probably just the strain of getting used to a whole new place," Elizabeth suggested.

Todd brightened again. "Yeah," he agreed. "That's probably it. Anyway, she seems to be doing OK." He bounced the ball off the sidewalk a few times, apparently lost in thought as the three of them reached the entrance to the cafeteria.

"Do you want to have lunch with us, Todd?" Nina invited.

"Huh?" he said, snapping back to earth. "Oh, thanks, but I need a shower. Anyway, I just stopped to tell you that I thought it was great what you did for Tom last night, Elizabeth."

"Really?" she asked, pleased. Todd and Tom had been at each other's throats for so long that a truce between them would be truly welcome.

"Yeah. I mean, finding the guy's father when

he didn't even know he had one—that's pretty spectacular."

"I'll say," Nina agreed.

Elizabeth could feel her face flushing with pleasure at her friends' unexpected praise. "Thanks," she said. "That means a lot."

"Yeah, well, I'll see you later," Todd said, bouncing the ball once off the cafeteria wall before he struck out toward the quad.

"Later," Elizabeth called to his back. She followed Nina into the comparative darkness of the cafeteria and all the way along the food line without being able to get Todd's new image out of her mind. The way he'd looked . . . like the Todd she *used* to know. The Todd she used to love. . . . She shook her head violently.

"Todd looked happy, don't you think?" Elizabeth asked Nina as they reached the cashier.

"More like ecstatic," Nina agreed, using Todd's own words.

"It's funny," Elizabeth said thoughtfully. "I think that's the happiest I've seen him since we all came to SVU."

"Definitely," Nina confirmed.

For the first time that day Elizabeth felt a trace of shadow cross her sun.

She knew she'd always care about Todd, and she wished him all the best. *So why does seeing him so happy bother me so much?* she wondered.

* * *

"You should have been there, Lila!" Jessica crowed, throwing herself backward in the overstuffed chair in a rapture of recollection. "It was so cool!"

Lila looked skeptical as she surveyed Jessica from her own chair in the Theta Alpha Theta parlor. The two girls were alone in the room, and Jessica was treating Lila to a blow-by-blow account of her morning adventures with Nick.

"It sounds a little . . . dangerous," Lila replied.

"Of course it was dangerous!" Jessica exclaimed. "That's what made it so fun! And then at the end, when he kissed me—"

"I get the picture," Lila interrupted, a bored tone creeping into her voice.

Jessica sat up, indignant. Lila was perched on the edge of a paisley chair like a very well-dressed stone, barely paying attention at all. The only part of her that even looked alive was the one delicate index finger that unconsciously twirled a strand of long, auburn hair. "Why are you in such a bad mood?" Jessica demanded.

"I'm not," Lila denied.

"No, not much," Jessica said. "I can't believe you. How can you sit there like you're about to fall asleep when I'm telling you something this big—no, this *huge?*"

Lila looked down at the lap of her expensive white linen suit. "All right," she admitted. "I guess I'm *not* in a very good mood."

"But why?" Jessica asked, scooting forward in her chair and studying her friend.

"It's stupid," Lila answered.

"What?"

"It's just that . . . well, Bruce's parents are having a formal outdoor brunch on Wednesday and we have to go."

Jessica laughed in disbelief. *"Brunch?"* she said. "You're upset about brunch?"

"Oh, sure," Lila returned sarcastically. "That's easy for you to say. The Patmans don't hate you."

"What are you talking about?" Jessica asked. "The Patmans love you."

"No, they don't," Lila said. "Not since Bruce and I moved in together."

"But that was ages ago," Jessica protested. "They must be over it by now."

Lila shook her head. "Sometimes I think they'll never get over it. You know how obsessed they are with the Patman reputation."

"The Fowler reputation is just as good!" Jessica said loyally.

Lila smiled. "Thanks," she said, "but Bruce's parents don't seem to think so. It's like I've put some kind of permanent blot on their record."

"You're paranoid," Jessica decided.

"I wish that were it," Lila said, "but things just aren't the same. Even though Bruce and I have been living apart for a while now, we're still walking on eggshells with his parents."

"So don't go to the brunch," Jessica recommended, losing interest and sinking back into her chair.

"I have to. It'll be even worse if I don't go." Lila looked truly miserable. "Oh, that reminds me," she added, "could you do me a huge favor?"

"Sure," Jessica answered. "Anything."

"I ordered the cutest hat to wear to the brunch with my new white dress. The problem is, it's not going to be finished until Tuesday evening, and I have a study group then that I can't afford to miss. Could you possibly pick it up for me?"

"Sure," Jessica said, barely listening. Who cared about boring things like brunches and hats when there were exciting guys like Nick Fox in the world?

"Thanks, Jess," Lila said, sounding relieved. "I know it's kind of dumb, but I really want to make a good impression on the Patmans."

"No problem," Jessica assured her.

Poor Lila's life was really getting dull . . . especially compared to Jessica's. She hugged herself with excitement as she thought about her date with Nick for that very night. Everything about him intrigued her—especially the secrecy. Not that he'd be keeping his secrets much longer. Jessica was going to make sure of that.

"Oh no." Lila groaned suddenly. "Just what we need."

Jessica tore herself away from her daydreams to

see Lila's eyes fixed on something outside the front window.

"What?" Jessica asked.

"You'll find out," Lila promised ominously, turning her chair slightly away from the front door.

A second later the door flew open, admitting Celine Boudreaux and a cloud of magnolia-scented perfume. As always, Celine looked like she was made up for a photo shoot, and every curl of her thick, honey-colored hair was beautifully arranged. The pink lace dress she had on would have looked ridiculous on anybody else, but Celine wore it with complete self-assurance, somehow managing to pull it off.

"Oh, perfect," Jessica whispered to Lila.

"Why, I declare," Celine drawled, piling on the southern accent with a shovel. "If it isn't Miss Personality and Miss Congeniality—I'll let y'all decide who's who."

"Shove off, Celine," Jessica growled.

"Oooh, that's no way to treat a *sister*," Celine admonished, crossing the room to stand over Jessica's chair. "Now that we're all going to be Thetas together, I guess you'll just have to work on your manners."

Lila looked up with barely concealed distaste. "If you'll recall, Celine," she said, "neither of us plans to vote for you."

Celine laughed, an artificial, tinkling little laugh that made Jessica want to strangle her.

"Well, now," she said, "I'll allow that I was hurt by that at first, but you know what? It doesn't matter one teensy little bit. I'm going to be a Theta, and there's nothing y'all can do about it."

"Celine?" a voice called from upstairs. "Is that you?"

"I do believe that's Alison calling me," Celine purred, heading for the stairs. "Coming, Alison." She paused at the top of the staircase just long enough to throw down one last triumphant glance before she ran off to pay homage to the Theta vice president, Alison Quinn.

"Those two were made for each other," Jessica said, disgusted, as Celine vanished from sight. Unfortunately there was no more love between Jessica and phony, snobby Alison Quinn than there was between her and Celine.

"No kidding," Lila agreed.

"I can't believe she's *buying* her way into the Thetas," Jessica continued. The sorority had agreed to hold a special house meeting to vote on Celine's admittance only after Celine's grandmother had offered to pay for the redecoration of the Theta parlor.

"Yeah," Lila said. "Especially since she hasn't even done what she promised yet." She gestured at the shabby old furnishings around them with an expression that spoke volumes.

Just then the front door opened again, admitting Denise Waters.

"What's up?" Denise asked, walking over to her friends. "You two look like you've been sucking lemons."

"Talking to Celine," Jessica corrected. "Common mistake."

Denise grimaced but then smiled bravely. "Maybe it won't be that bad. Maybe Celine's turned over a new leaf. Maybe she won't even get in," Denise added hopefully.

Jessica looked at Lila, and their skeptical eyes locked. "She won't if I have anything to say about it."

Chapter Three

Nick pushed his way through some dense red hibiscus bushes, then struck out across the grass of the athletics training fields. Normally he wasn't quite so cautious, but the phone call he had to make was too important to risk having any of it overheard. There were a few guys on the fields playing tag football, but that didn't bother Nick. The athletes were too busy mauling each other to pay any attention to a guy on a cell phone, and the noise they made would help keep anyone else from listening.

Selecting a place near the sidelines, right out in the open, Nick dialed a number he knew by heart. It rang only twice.

"Sweet Valley Police Department," said an efficient voice on the other end.

"Hey, Sheila, it's Nick. How about letting me speak to the captain?"

"Hi, Nick! Sure thing."

Nick waited through the usual clicks, buzzes, and Musak before Captain Wallace finally picked up the call.

"Captain Wallace!" the chief barked ferociously, as if he thought someone was likely to dispute it.

"Hi, Chief," Nick said, relieved to hear his boss's voice. "I'm afraid I've got some bad news."

"Then let's hear it, Fox," the captain said. "I don't have all day."

Nick allowed himself to smile from the safety of the other end of the phone. The chief loved to act like a real tough guy, but everyone knew he was a total pushover.

"Somebody ID'ed me today," Nick told the captain. "It was pretty close."

"Is your cover blown?" the chief asked immediately. "I'm bringing you in."

"No, I'm still OK. But they *did* take me on one hell of a wild ride." Nick had planned to tell Captain Wallace the entire story, but for some reason he was suddenly reluctant to mention Jessica's involvement.

"So who was it?" Captain Wallace asked.

"Remember the DeMarco brothers?" Nick replied. "Apparently they're still upset about being one DeMarco short."

Captain Wallace chuckled with satisfaction. "Jackie DeMarco," he said. "I hated that little sleaze. The best thing you ever did was put him in jail."

"Yeah, well, his fan club doesn't agree. You're going to have to pick those guys up, Chief."

"My pleasure," Captain Wallace said. "What are they driving these days?"

"You won't believe it—that same old black Cadillac. The guys are total geniuses."

"What do you expect?" the chief joked. "They're drug dealers, not brain surgeons."

"Yeah," Nick said. "The brain surgery patients of the world can be grateful for that. Anyway, they're definitely out to get me."

"Don't give it another thought," Captain Wallace ordered. "I'll have those losers picked up by nightfall. You just keep a low profile and let's get this job finished right."

"Thanks, Chief," Nick said. "That's what I'm here for."

"Are you sure your cover isn't blown?" the chief asked again. He sounded strangely concerned.

"Of course," Nick said. "I mean, those guys already knew me." A nagging little voice at the back of his mind was asking what Jessica must think, but Nick chose to ignore it.

"Well, I'm glad to hear it," Captain Wallace said, "because *I've* got some bad news for *you*. We lost John Doe."

Nick groaned loudly. They'd spent weeks

building that connection. "How?" he asked.

"Don't know. The guy just disappeared. The thing is, our boys in the field thought he had a meeting with you last night."

"With me?" Nick repeated, confused. "No."

"He never called you for a pickup?" the chief asked.

"No," Nick insisted.

"I don't know what happened, then," Captain Wallace said. "We'll have to keep working on it."

"What a nightmare," Nick moaned. "If we don't find him, we'll have to start from scratch."

"Tell me about it," the chief agreed. "Better get on it, Fox."

"Right, Captain." Nick clicked off the phone.

After he'd hung up, Nick stood on the sidelines a minute, trying to comprehend what had happened. Was it possible that his cover *was* blown and that the man who called himself John Doe had somehow been tipped to the fact that his new customer was really a cop? Nick shook his head—he didn't see how. Discouraged, he began making his way back across the athletics fields toward the dorms.

All that work for nothing! he thought. It would probably take weeks to come up with another contact as good as John Doe. At this rate Nick could be at SVU forever. The glimmer of a smile crossed Nick's scowling face. It had just occurred to him that there was *one* thing about that scenario that wouldn't be completely terrible—more time with Jessica Wakefield. *Oh, man,* he scolded himself, smiling in earnest. *You should* not *be thinking like that.*

But now that he'd started, he couldn't stop. *After all,* he reasoned, *a college boy has to have a college girlfriend, right?* Before he thought another second, Nick whipped the cellular phone back out of his pocket and punched in Jessica's number.

"Hello?" Jessica answered.

"Hi. It's Nick." He could tell he had a ridiculous grin on his face as he stopped under a group of palm trees to talk to her, but he didn't care.

"Nick!" Jessica exclaimed. "What's the matter?"

"What do you mean?" he asked, alarmed. How would Jessica know something was the matter?

"I mean, we're still going out tonight, aren't we?" she asked.

"Oh, you bet," Nick assured her, relieved. "I just couldn't wait that long to talk to you."

Jessica giggled happily, and Nick felt his heart flip over. Nick knew the effect Jessica had on him wasn't good. In fact, it was very, very bad. Jessica was only a contact, another way to get to know the main players on campus. He wasn't supposed to get attached to her.

"I want to take you somewhere quiet tonight,"

he blurted. "Somewhere we can be alone together." *Way to distance yourself, Fox,* the still-sane portion of his mind mocked him.

"I'd like that," Jessica said, her voice hinting at all the delicious possibilities such an arrangement would offer.

By the time Nick got off the phone, his head was swimming. Was he nuts to be dating her? Should they cool it? "I'm not going to think about it," he resolved aloud, pushing the conflict of interest from his mind. Jessica made him feel terrific—he wanted to be near her.

A carefully tousled blond hairdo caught Nick's eye as he returned the phone to his pocket. The hairdo's owner was sauntering along the walkway next to the student center, wearing stiletto heels and a pink lace dress. "Celine," he said with a groan, coming back to earth. With the John Doe contact out of the picture, Nick was going to have to follow up on all those not-so-subtle hints Celine had been dropping since he'd first met her.

"Great," he muttered, envisioning Jessica's reaction. Nick himself had been immediately put off by Celine's phony attitude, but Jessica had a major problem with her. If she caught him talking to her enemy without looking as if he were hating every minute of it, she was going be furious. Unfortunately Nick couldn't think of a way to avoid it. As unlikely as Celine was to come up with anything useful, he had no other leads to go on at the moment.

I'll talk to Celine tomorrow, Nick decided, watching her disappear into the student center before he took off in the opposite direction. *And if I'm lucky, Jessica won't find out.*

Celine peered intently around the dark interior of the student center. Compared to being in the glare outside, walking into the center was like entering a cave, but Celine barely noticed as she stood inside the door, casting around for a target.

He has to be smart enough, but not too smart, she thought as she sized up the candidates appraisingly. *Not too cute either. But he can't be disgusting, of course.* Celine's blue eyes roamed the enormous room, skipping from guy to guy. The pickings were as slim as they'd been when she'd checked earlier that morning, and Celine felt herself beginning to panic.

Everything depended on this plan. Her induction into Theta Alpha Theta, her reentry into SVU society, everything. In order to convince the Thetas to let her join their sorority, Celine had promised that her granny Boudreaux would pay to redecorate the parlor. Unfortunately the selfish old hag had refused to cooperate. So now it was up to Celine to come up with the necessary thousands of dollars—and quickly too, before the Thetas got suspicious.

Celine had been prepared for the likelihood that her grandmother wouldn't help her, and she'd already taken steps to start raising the money herself. The problem was, she couldn't pull off her moneymaking plan alone. If she were to get caught . . . Celine shivered involuntarily in the warm, climate-controlled air of the student center. Getting caught wasn't an option.

Hello! Celine suddenly interrupted her own thoughts, focusing with interest on a guy reading a student newspaper on the other side of the room. He was sitting on an ugly vinyl sofa by himself, apparently trying to blend into the wallpaper. A blue baseball cap with an oversize brim was pulled low over his eyes, and he held the newspaper awkwardly out in front of him so that it covered most of the rest of his face. *Shy,* Celine thought. *Perfect.*

She walked seductively across the room in his direction, getting halfway there before she realized she was wasting her time—his eyes were glued to the news. Annoyed, Celine hurried the rest of the distance to his side and dropped lightly onto the tacky couch beside him.

"Excuse me," she said in a breathless voice that was only half acting—her nerves were making her heart pound like crazy. "Do you mind if I sit here?"

Celine's mark looked up from his newspaper and did a very satisfying double take. She could practically *hear* him sweat as he realized that a beautiful girl was talking to *him*.

"No!" he blurted, flushing as he struggled to fold his resisting newspaper. "Go ahead!" He gave up trying to fold it and wrestled the paper into a disordered heap in his lap.

"Well, now, aren't you sweet?" Celine smiled, leaning back into the sofa and stretching her arms up behind her head in a way designed to show her many assets. "What's your name, sugar?"

"Jordan," he answered, his sky blue eyes popping at the sight of Celine's lace-clad figure. "Jordan Wilson."

For a moment Celine almost changed her mind. Those eyes—they were so close to the color William White's had been. William, her one true love. A wave of sickening regret threatened to overwhelm her. *He's dead, Celine,* she reminded herself harshly. *And more than a little responsible for getting you into this mess in the first place.* If only she'd realized how sick William was! Celine had known that William's obsession with Elizabeth Wakefield wasn't normal, of course, but she'd never believed that he'd actually try to kill his little princess. And Celine, blinded by love, had been dragged smack into the middle of the whole sordid affair—right up until the time that William had tried to kill her too.

She still wished she could pay William back for everything he'd done to her, and especially for the way he'd used her. *On second thought,* Celine decided vindictively, imagining William's face superimposed on Jordan's, *those ice blue eyes are kind of a plus.* She could always pretend that she was finally getting her revenge.

"Pleased to meet you, Jordan Wilson," she drawled, hoping he was into southern. Then again, she'd never met a guy who wasn't. She extended her right hand toward his. "Celine Boudreaux."

Jordan simply stared, transfixed, before he suddenly seemed to get it. "Oh!" he exclaimed, lunging for her hand so abruptly that pages of his forgotten newspaper were launched all over the linoleum. "Glad to meet you too." He pumped her hand so earnestly that Celine didn't have to entirely fake her smile.

He wasn't that bad looking, really. Nerdy, of course, but not beyond redemption. Very short, white blond hair blended with his bleached blue eyes, but thick, dark lashes and a sprinkling of freckles kept Jordan's face from fading into paleness. That and the ruddy, excited flush he wore on his cheeks. *A few days in the sun . . .* she found herself thinking. Celine shook her head impatiently and called herself back to the matter at hand.

"Well, now, Jordan," she said, gently extracting her fingers from his overly enthusiastic grip. "How come I haven't seen you around here before?"

Jordan sat back and wiped his palms against his jeans. "Probably because I just started school," he answered. "I'm a freshman."

"Really?" Celine knew that no one could have looked more shocked than she did, even though she could barely keep from screaming, *No kidding!*

"I would have guessed you were a junior at least," she lied, inching her way closer on the couch.

Jordan puffed up noticeably inside his roomy, blue-striped button-down. "A lot of people think I'm older than I am," he confided.

"I can see why," Celine murmured, already losing interest in a game that challenged her so little. Still, she needed this guy. Badly.

"You know," she added suddenly, as if she had just that minute thought of it, "this is all so abrupt—and I sure hope you won't take it the wrong way—but . . . well, would you like to have lunch with me tomorrow? You can say no if you want to," she assured him, hoping she sounded appropriately embarrassed. "I know this is awfully forward of me—"

"Not at all," Jordan rushed to interrupt her.

"I don't want you to think that I do this all the time or anything," Celine told him, putting her hand over his on the sofa and leaning in to gaze up at him with wide, innocent eyes. "It's just that you seem so nice. I'd like to get to know you better."

"Uh, thank you," Jordan managed, clearly flabbergasted. "Lunch sounds good."

"You know something?" Celine continued in a confiding tone of voice. "The second I saw you sitting over here, I had a feeling that you and I were going to be good friends."

Jordan started to puff up again, but then shrugged it off and glanced down at the floor, like a man with no illusions. He knew what he was, Celine realized with a rush of certainty. Good—it would make her job that much easier.

"I don't usually have such a desirable effect on women," Jordan admitted.

"Well, you look just about *perfect* to me, sugar," Celine told him truthfully. "Now, lend me a pencil and I'll give you my address."

Alex wandered in the direction of her dorm room, happier than she'd been in days. Doug had let her shadow his calls well into the afternoon, and as she walked alone across the sunny, peaceful campus Alex saw in her mind's eye only the phone-line lights flashing in the cramped, dingy phone room of the hot line. The calls she had monitored still echoed in her ears.

"How do you know when you have a problem?"

"I didn't want to, but . . ."

"Sometimes it seems like this stuff is taking over my life."

Alex knew what it felt like to be desperate enough to call a total stranger for help. When she'd been drinking, she'd been every bit that desperate and more. Thankfully Noah had helped her.

"And I can help *these* people," she told herself out loud, pushing the painful memory of Noah from her mind. "I can, and I will."

A feeling of exhilaration came over Alex as she spoke her promise. For the first time in a long while she had a purpose—a reason to get up in the morning more compelling than going shopping or attending the latest sorority function. Alex lifted her chin and walked a little prouder. She'd made her share of mistakes—no doubt about that—but she was putting them behind her now. From now on the world was going to see a new, stronger Alex. She'd already reinvented herself once, at the beginning of college when she'd changed her name from Enid and become the glamorous, popular Alex Rollins. Now she would do it again.

I just wish I didn't have to do it alone, she thought, dropping her chin once more.

"Tom!" Elizabeth exclaimed, surprised and pleased. "I didn't think you were coming by until later."

She opened the door of the dorm room she

and Jessica shared a little wider. "Come on in," she urged, taking him by the wrist and drawing him inside. "Where's Mr. Conroy?"

"Hello, beautiful," Tom said, pausing to kiss her appreciatively before he answered her question. "He's outside in the car."

"In the car! Why didn't you invite him in?" Elizabeth was halfway back out the door before Tom could stop her.

"Chill out," he said with a laugh. "I didn't abandon him or anything. In fact, we're on our way now to see all the glorious sights of Sweet Valley. I just wanted to catch you before we left to make sure you'd go to dinner with us tonight."

Elizabeth was confused. "But I thought your father was going back to L.A. early."

"He was," Tom confirmed, "but now he wants to stay a little longer and take us out to dinner. You will go, won't you?"

"I don't know if I should," Elizabeth worried. "I mean, I don't want to intrude—"

"Intrude?" Tom cut her off. "Liz, if it weren't for you, I wouldn't even know about him. I can't tell you what it means to me to . . . well, to know that I'm not alone anymore. I have a father! *And* a brother and sister. And I owe it all to you."

Elizabeth waved him off modestly and sat in her desk chair. Tom took a seat across from her on the bed, but the room was so small, they could still hold hands. "I'm so glad you're happy," she told him, putting her entire heart into the words as she gazed into his handsome face.

Tom smiled, and the skin at the corners of his brown eyes crinkled. "You have no idea. Mr. Conroy—uh, I mean, George—could never replace my first dad, but it's just so incredible to have a father at all, you know?"

Elizabeth nodded.

"After my family died in the accident . . ." Tom shook off the memory. "I just never thought I'd be happy in the same way again."

"I think it's terrific," Elizabeth encouraged him, taking both his hands in hers.

"Me too," Tom said. "It's still a little weird—don't get me wrong—but I know this is going to be a lifelong relationship. Maybe we'll never truly feel like father and son, but there's something special between us." Tom laughed, seemingly embarrassed by the way he'd been running on. "Right now it's more like a mutual admiration society."

"Why not?" Elizabeth teased, smiling. "I admire you often."

Tom leaned forward and brushed his lips across her cheek. "You nut," he said with a smile. "So are you going to dinner with us or what?"

"Sure. If you really want me to."

"Are you kidding?" Tom squeezed her hands

and held her gaze solemnly. "Elizabeth, I always wanted to have my family love you as much as I do. Now I finally have the chance."

Elizabeth was so moved, she felt tears burn her eyes as she held tightly to Tom's hands. "Of course I'll go," she said shakily.

Tom pulled her from the chair onto his lap and folded her into his strong arms. "Hey," he said gently. "Don't cry."

"I'm just so happy," she managed, smiling through her tears. "I'm not really crying."

"No. Not much." Tom brought his lips to her face, kissing away each tear in turn as he smoothed her silky hair. "You're so incredible, Elizabeth. When we walk into that restaurant tonight, every guy in the room is going to wish he were me."

"You're exaggerating," she protested, but she was pleased all the same. It wasn't such an unpleasant mental picture.

"I'll bet I'm not," Tom said with a faraway look in his eyes, as if he were already there, witnessing the entire scene.

"And besides," he added, coming back to the present, "George will be crushed if you don't go with us. As far as my father's concerned, I'm starting to think you walk on water."

Elizabeth giggled and pushed her way out of Tom's lap. "I really like your father," she said.

"And *he* really likes *you*. Can we pick you up

around six-thirty?" Tom waited for her answer expectantly.

"Sure," she agreed. "How fancy should I dress?"

Tom shrugged. "Better go all out," he recommended. "I have a feeling George has a big night planned."

Chapter Four

Jessica held Nick's hand with something less than total enthusiasm as they stood in line to buy tickets for the early show. Of course she was glad to be out with him again, but the movies didn't exactly fit her idea of a big night out. She looked down at her sheer white blouse and flowing blue silk pants and felt conspicuously overdressed.

"I thought you said we were going somewhere *quiet,*" Jessica ventured at last. "I thought you wanted to be alone with me."

Nick turned and smiled mischievously. "We'll sit in the back. And believe me, when the lights go out, I'll make you forget there's anyone else in the room."

Jessica smiled back in spite of herself. It was the kind of thing people did in high school, but she supposed it could be fun. Besides, they were going to see the very first show—there would still be time to talk Nick into something more romantic later on. She looked him over discreetly as they waited their turn to buy tickets. He was wearing jeans, motorcycle boots, a red T-shirt, and a black leather jacket. He looked hot, and Jessica felt the familiar thrill at the thought that this gorgeous, mysterious man was interested in her. *On second thought,* Jessica said to herself, *making out in the movies could be* very *fun.*

"Besides," Nick added, totally oblivious to her thoughts. "I thought it would be nice to do something normal and boring for a change. Didn't you get enough excitement before breakfast this morning?"

"I don't believe you're capable of being boring," Jessica told him. She let go of his hand and took his arm instead, drawing herself in tight against his body. "And I *never* get enough excitement."

Nick responded by pulling her into his arms and kissing her deeply. "Excitement is a bad habit," he warned huskily.

"You're not doing anything to help me get over it," Jessica said, kissing him back.

For a moment they lost themselves kissing on the sidewalk in plain, public view, but gradually Jessica remembered where they were. She drew her lips away from Nick's and looked up into his half closed eyes. She was falling for this guy, she realized. She was falling hard, and she didn't even know who he was.

"What's your secret, Nick?" she asked for the second time that day. "You can't keep me in the dark forever."

Nick opened his eyes. They looked worried, conflicted. "No," he agreed. "And I don't *want* to keep you in the dark."

"Then tell me!" Jessica begged.

"I would if I could," he said earnestly. "But there are too many things you wouldn't understand."

Jessica let go of him and faced him down with her hands on her hips. "That's my whole point," she said irritably. "I *can't* understand—because you won't let me. I thought you liked me."

"I do," Nick said earnestly. "Jessica, try to be patient. I'll tell you as soon as I possibly can."

"Tell me now," she suggested, her blue eyes intense.

"Jessica . . ."

Nick looked like a beaten man, and Jessica felt a thrill of pure adrenaline. He was going to cave—she knew the signs.

"Yes, Nick?" she said sweetly, gazing up into his face.

"He's got a gun!" The sudden, panicked scream from a woman near the front of the line ripped through the mellow evening. Jessica could barely take in what was happening as the line before them scattered in all directions, away from the box office. In the clearing Jessica saw that only feet away a filthy, desperate-looking man held a gun on the cashier through the hole of the ticket window.

"Get down!" Nick ordered, pushing Jessica hard to one side and springing forward toward the gunman.

"Nick!" Jessica screamed. He'd be killed!

Like someone caught in a dream, Jessica watched, motionless, as the gunman whirled to point his weapon at Nick's charging form. The terrified teenage boy behind the cash register immediately took advantage of the commotion and dropped to the ground.

"Nick! No!" It didn't even sound like her voice.

The gun was coming around. In another split second . . .

Nick's right hand chopped down on the gunman's forearm so forcefully that Jessica could barely follow the blurred motion. The handgun flew from the man's grasp and clattered against the concrete. Moving quickly and precisely, Nick stepped in front of the robber and delivered a punishing upward blow to the chin. The gunman's head snapped back and he dropped forward to his knees. With a quick push of Nick's foot the criminal was down on his face.

"Don't move," Nick warned calmly, putting a knee in the man's back and twisting his gun arm into an unnatural position behind his neck. "Or I'll break your arm."

The whole thing had taken only seconds.

"Nick!" Jessica rushed forward, wanting to touch him, to make sure he was really alive.

"Get back, Jessica," he said sharply. "I don't want you anywhere near this creep."

Jessica reluctantly took one step backward.

"Don't worry, everyone! I've called the police!" The theater manager came rushing through the main glass doors of the not-yet-open lobby, yelling as he ran. Two strong-looking college-age ushers followed hard behind him. "Everyone, please stay calm," the manager directed the crowd. "Everything's under control."

Jessica watched the ushers help Nick force the gunman to his feet and drag him through the glass doors into the empty lobby to wait for the police. The theater manager stayed behind on the pavement outdoors, checking to make sure that none of his customers were hurt.

"That was my boyfriend who just caught that guy," Jessica said, walking up to the manager and pointing in the direction Nick had gone. "I want to go with him."

The manager immediately straightened up from where he'd been stooping to reassure a frightened child. "Your boyfriend?" he repeated, grabbing her hand and shaking it hard. "You must be incredibly proud of him." The manager was in his forties, Jessica guessed, with a friendly smile and curly, graying black hair.

"Well, right now I'm more worried than anything else," Jessica admitted. "If we could go inside . . ."

"Of course." The manager took Jessica's arm and led her toward the lobby, holding the heavy glass door open for her. Inside the lobby Nick was leaning against the candy counter—alone.

"Nick!" Jessica exclaimed, rushing into his arms. "Are you OK?"

"Fine." He held her at arm's length and studied her face. "How about you?"

"I'm fine. No one outside was hurt." Jessica glanced around the deserted lobby. "What did you do with that stickup guy?"

Nick shrugged. "The ushers are keeping him in an office in back until the cops come."

The manager cleared his throat to get Nick's attention, then he stepped forward toward the couple. "I'd just like to thank you," he said, extending his hand and pumping Nick's. "Times are hard enough without getting ripped off too. Not only that, someone could have been killed if you hadn't reacted so quickly."

"It was nothing," Nick said, clearly embarrassed.

"Nothing!" The manager looked appalled. "You're a hero! As soon as the police get here that's exactly what I'll tell them too. Here," he added, slipping around behind the candy counter, "have some Jujyfruits on me."

Nick laughed. "I couldn't."

"Of course you could," Jessica told him, holding out her hand for the candy. "You *are* a hero, Nick."

"That's right," agreed the manager. "Don't

even think about buying tickets, of course. And if you want drinks, popcorn—anything—it's all on the house."

Jessica couldn't help smiling as the theater manager insisted on pressing more candy and snacks on a weakly protesting Nick, stuffing his jacket pockets until they bulged.

"Uh, could I speak to you alone for a minute?" Nick finally asked the manager.

"Of course!" The manager cast one brief, confused glance at Jessica, then led Nick to the other side of the lobby.

Jessica was left standing by the candy counter with an enormous box of Jujyfruits in her hands, wondering what Nick was saying. She could see the manager's face clearly, but Nick was doing all the talking and he had his back to her. The manager nodded a lot, apparently in total agreement with whatever Nick was telling him. A couple of minutes later the manager turned and walked out a side door, leaving Nick and Jessica alone in the lobby.

"Well," Nick said, rejoining Jessica. "That's all taken care of." He smiled broadly, sauntered behind the candy counter, and held up a huge paper cup. "May I offer you a soda, miss?" he asked with exaggerated courtesy.

"Nick! *What's* all taken care of?" Jessica protested as Nick filled the cup with ice from a bin with a sliding steel door.

"That guy. The manager's going to tell the police

what happened so we don't have to wait around for them. Diet Coke or diet Pepsi?"

Jessica shook her head in disbelief. "Don't *you* want to tell the police what happened?"

"Nope." Nick put the cup under the diet Coke spigot and pushed the button to fill it, at the same time turning to fill another cup with ice.

"But why not?"

Nick grinned, leaning forward over the counter. "Because why would I want to waste the next half hour talking to a bunch of guys when I could be spending it in a darkened theater completely alone with you?"

Jessica felt a jolt of excitement as she imagined what the half hour before the theater opened would be like. *And Nick thought the movies would be boring,* she remembered. How could they be? Nick was easily the most *un*boring guy she'd ever met.

"Oh, Mr. Conroy!" Elizabeth gasped as he steered his gold Mercedes around the last twisting curve and their destination came into view. "You shouldn't have!"

Tom's father smiled happily at Elizabeth before he began the descent down the long gravel drive to the restaurant below. "I'm glad you like it," he said, briefly removing a hand from the steering wheel to pat hers fondly. "And I definitely should have."

"Jessica will just die when I tell her about this."

Elizabeth turned to whisper to Tom over the back of the passenger seat, her blue-green eyes huge with excitement. "I can't believe we're having dinner at Andre's."

"I know," Tom agreed. His own eyes felt almost as big as Elizabeth's. "I thought you practically had to know the Pope to get into this place."

Tom had already guessed that Mr. Conroy was going to take them somewhere fancy—that was why he and Elizabeth were so dressed up—but Andre's was a Sweet Valley legend. Very expensive and even more exclusive, the celebrated French restaurant was completely out of the question for the average SVU student. Tom had never been there before, and neither had Elizabeth. No one Tom knew well had.

"It's exactly like I imagined it would be," Elizabeth told Mr. Conroy excitedly as they came to the end of the long private drive. The Mercedes stopped at the red carpet outside the entry to the low, sprawling building. They actually had a red carpet. And valets, of course. Two of them hustled over to open doors on both sides of the vehicle and escort the trio through the wide, hardwood doors marked only with a capital *A*.

"Allow me," Mr. Conroy said gallantly, taking Elizabeth's arm. She smiled up at the older man, and Tom felt a sudden rush of pride. Mr. Conroy looked stable and prosperous in his well-tailored suit, and Elizabeth clearly liked him a lot. Her left hand rested comfortably in the crook of his arm as the happy group passed through the massive doorway.

Inside, things were even more deluxe. Tom held Elizabeth's hand in the opulent atrium while Mr. Conroy checked their reservation with the maître d'. The elegant dining room was full to capacity with men in tuxedos and women in evening gowns. Even the waiters were wearing tuxedos, Tom noticed uncomfortably, glad he'd at least worn his best suit. Elizabeth squeezed his hand, as if she were reading his mind.

"If you'll all come this way . . . ," the maître d' said, stepping out from behind his station to lead them to their table.

"Ladies first," Mr. Conroy said, motioning for Tom and Elizabeth to go in front.

Tom held Elizabeth tightly by the hand as they stepped out into the glittering dining room. It was like entering another world—a world of incredible wealth and unquestioned privilege. Tom knew without asking that the elaborate chandeliers overhead were lead crystal, that the candles on the tables were beeswax, that the diamonds on the women were real. As the headwaiter led them to their table Tom stole a look at Elizabeth.

Elizabeth wore a strapless black velvet dress that Tom had never seen before, and her shining blond hair was styled in a sophisticated French twist. Her long skirt just barely grazed the plush, wine-colored carpeting as she walked at his side, her head held proudly. She was truly beautiful, Tom realized with a pang. The most beautiful woman there.

"You should have diamonds," he whispered, bending toward her ear. "They're wasted on everyone else."

The radiant smile Elizabeth gave him in return took his breath away.

"Your table, sir," said the maître d'. He pulled out a chair for Elizabeth and seated her facing into the room before assisting Tom and Mr. Conroy. "May I present your waiter, Aaron?" he added as a second man approached the table.

"Good evening," Aaron greeted them as the maître d' slipped away across the dining room.

"Good evening," everyone echoed politely. Tom felt as if he were on a 1940s movie set—everything was almost too perfect.

"Will you be drinking wine tonight?" the waiter asked Mr. Conroy solicitously. "We have an excellent wine list."

I'll just bet you do, Tom thought, afraid to imagine what a glass of wine must cost at a place like Andre's.

"Champagne, I think," Mr. Conroy answered. "What type do you recommend?"

Aaron smiled. "Of course the Dom Pérignon is very good."

Of course, Tom thought, smiling wryly at Elizabeth. Dom Pérignon was probably the most expensive champagne in the house.

"Fine." Mr. Conroy nodded. "Bring us the bottle."

Tom gasped.

"Very good, sir." The waiter bowed formally

and went off in search of the champagne.

"What's the matter, Tom?" Mr. Conroy asked, beaming at him and Elizabeth. "Don't you like champagne?"

"Yeah," Tom sputtered, "of course. But George, that bottle's probably going to cost—"

Mr. Conroy held up his hand for silence. "Tonight's a special night," he said. "After all, it isn't every night you get to treat your long-lost son and his beautiful girlfriend to dinner."

Elizabeth smiled modestly, and Tom stopped himself from protesting further. Elizabeth was so obviously pleased to be there, to see things going well between him and his father. And if it hadn't been for her . . .

No matter how much it costs, Tom decided, *Elizabeth deserves this night.* There was no way either he or his father could ever repay her for bringing them together. "Thank you," he told Mr. Conroy gratefully.

"My pleasure," Mr. Conroy replied. "So what will you have?" he added, turning to smile at Elizabeth. "I'm told that the lobster here is very good."

"I pretty much like the lobster everywhere," Elizabeth admitted, laughing. "But I was thinking of trying one of these French specialties of the house."

Tom watched in a happy glow as his father and Elizabeth consulted the elaborate menu. Finally, after years of misery, his life was getting back on track. For so long it had seemed that he was alone, cut loose in the world. Of course he'd had Elizabeth, but a girlfriend wasn't the same thing as family. Tom had wished so desperately for some roots, a family he could share with Elizabeth, and now—unbelievably—that wish had come true.

Mr. Conroy looked up from his menu as Aaron delivered the champagne in a gleaming silver bucket, uncorked it, and began decanting it into crystal champagne flutes.

"I shouldn't," Elizabeth murmured, holding up her hand to stop the waiter from pouring champagne for her.

"Just one glass," George urged, motioning to Aaron to fill all three anyway. "For the toast."

Elizabeth gave in. "Well, OK. If we're toasting."

"Of course we're toasting," Mr. Conroy pronounced, lifting his glass high. "Come on, you two."

Tom smiled as he lifted his own glass. After all, he was newly twenty-one, and he had plenty to celebrate. Elizabeth joined him, her slender fingers raising her glass next to his.

"To Tom," Mr. Conroy proposed. "And to making up for lost time."

"To Tom," Elizabeth echoed.

Incredibly, Tom felt himself blushing. He tried to say something, to make a joke, but his throat was tight with emotion. In the end he simply clinked his glass blindly against the others and sipped the expensive champagne. When he put his drink back on the table, Tom was almost overwhelmed again by the tender looks in Elizabeth's and his father's eyes.

"There's something else I've been waiting to tell you," Mr. Conroy said, removing an envelope from his inside jacket pocket and pushing it across the table toward Tom. "The details are in here, but the short version is that you have a trust fund."

"A trust fund?" Tom managed, shocked.

His father nodded. "It's not a fortune, but you'll never have to worry. I started it for you the day your mother left me." He reached across the table, gripping Tom's wrist. "I know I messed up, Tom—I've known it all your life. But if you'll let me, I want to be there for you now."

"Wow," Tom said at last, putting the envelope into his jacket pocket with a shaking hand. "I feel like I just won the lottery or something."

Mr. Conroy laughed. "In a way, I guess you did."

"No," Tom hurried to clarify. "I don't mean because of the money—although I . . . I can't thank you enough for that. I mean, everything. Being with you, George, I mean."

"Call me Dad," Mr. Conroy encouraged, his voice shaking slightly. "That is, if you want to."

Tom nodded, unable to speak, and traces of tears glistened in both men's eyes. Tom couldn't call George "Dad"—not yet. But he had the feeling he'd be able to very, very soon.

* * *

Elizabeth watched the scene between Tom and his father play out with a full heart. Her own eyes streamed unheeded as she watched Tom struggle to choke back tears of joy.

He deserves it, she thought happily. *More than anyone I know.*

"Are you ready to order?" asked their waiter, Aaron, appearing silently out of nowhere. "Oh, I'll come back," he apologized quickly, noticing Elizabeth's teary face.

"No, that's OK," she said, dabbing at her cheeks with a white linen napkin, but the waiter had already vanished.

"I think I'll take a quick trip to the men's room anyway," Tom husked, standing.

Elizabeth knew he was making an excuse to leave the table in order to regain his self-control, but it only made her love him more. She smiled at his back as he retreated across the dining room.

Mr. Conroy didn't seem fooled either. "Is he always so reserved?" he asked, sipping his champagne. The tears that had sparkled in his eyes only moments before had been replaced by a look of amusement.

Elizabeth nodded, meeting his gaze. "That was actually a major display of emotion for Tom. He takes things to heart."

"I was getting that impression. He's just like his old man."

Mr. Conroy smiled at her, and Elizabeth felt another rush of happiness—for both men. Maybe she was imagining it, but she was even starting to see a resemblance between them. They were both built tall and strong, and if Mr. Conroy's receding brown hair was lighter and thinner than Tom's, his dark brown eyes were just as expressive.

"I can't stress enough how much having you in his life means to Tom," she said. "And I know he's looking forward to meeting his brother and sister too. I can honestly say that I've never seen him happier."

"We both have you to thank for that," Mr. Conroy said, putting his hand over hers on the table. "You know, when I set out to look for Tom, I never imagined I'd find someone as beautiful as you, Elizabeth."

Elizabeth dropped her eyes, embarrassed. "Thank you," she murmured self-consciously.

"I can see you don't believe me," Mr. Conroy said. "But I'm serious."

Elizabeth nodded, unsure how to respond. No doubt he meant it kindly, but the compliment seemed a little too emphatic.

"Tom was right, you know," he continued. "You *should* have diamonds. You're the most exquisite woman in the room."

Mr. Conroy had listened to their private conversation? Elizabeth felt a hot blush spreading across her cheeks.

"Of course, boys Tom's age don't usually spend their money on gems, so I'm afraid you'll have to do without them for a while." Mr. Conroy laughed, as if a thought had suddenly occurred to him. "That is, unless you're planning on replacing him sometime soon," he added.

Elizabeth couldn't believe her ears. Replace Tom? *Mr. Conroy must be joking,* she told herself, but his remark made her uncomfortable just the same. Not only that, his hand was still resting on hers on the table. Hadn't it been there a little too long?

"I think I'll keep him—at least for a while," Elizabeth bantered weakly, wishing he'd change the subject.

"Too bad." Mr. Conroy reached for the champagne bottle with his free hand and refilled Elizabeth's glass. *Now why did he do that?* she asked herself. *He knows I don't want any more.*

"I don't suppose you'd ever consider dating an old codger like me?" he asked, squeezing her fingers slightly.

Elizabeth was dumbfounded. He was kidding. Wasn't he? "Maybe if I wasn't already dating your son," she replied, trying to laugh it off.

"Drink your champagne," Mr. Conroy encouraged.

Elizabeth seized the excuse to remove her hand from under his, placing it around the cool crystal of her champagne flute instead. She noticed that the glass trembled slightly as she brought it to her lips.

"So, did I miss anything?" Tom asked jovially, returning to the table.

"Not a thing," Mr. Conroy said smoothly. "We were just waiting for you to get back before we ordered. What'll you have, son?"

"I don't know," Tom answered, smiling. "What's the most expensive thing on the menu?"

Mr. Conroy laughed heartily, and Tom joined him. "You're a man after my own heart," Tom's father said, clapping his son on the back. "Let's look into that."

Elizabeth watched as the two men pored over the menu together, looking for the most outrageous delicacy on it. A few minutes before she would have been laughing along with them, but now everything felt strange and uncomfortable. Had Mr. Conroy really been kidding around, or had he been propositioning her? The thought made her sick. How could he do that to Tom?

"What are you having, Liz?" Tom asked suddenly, his face flushed with laughter. "Think big— it's all on George!"

Mr. Conroy was kidding, Elizabeth decided, forcing every other possibility from her mind. Looking into Tom's happy, trusting eyes, she knew it was the only explanation she could stand. Mr. Conroy hadn't just come on to her. He was kidding, and that was that.

Chapter Five

"Wake up, sleepyhead! The early bird gets up early and all that junk."

"Jessica?" Elizabeth removed the covers from her puffy, half-dazed face. "What are you doing up?"

Jessica stood over her sleep-befuddled twin. "It's seven o'clock. While you're just lying there, the whole day's a-wasting!"

Jessica couldn't help smiling at Elizabeth's confused, annoyed expression. It was fun to do this to someone for a change, instead of having it done to her. Not only that, for once Elizabeth had come in from a date really late, which just made waking her up at such an unnatural hour of the morning that much more rewarding.

"Why are you doing this?" Elizabeth grumbled, sitting up in bed and reaching for her bathrobe. "Were you replaced by aliens or something? I can't believe you're up early two mornings in a row."

Jessica sat on her own bed, facing her twin. "It seems like we never get to *talk* anymore," she said melodramatically, lifting some dialogue from her favorite soap opera. The truth was that she couldn't wait to tell Elizabeth about the way Nick had handled that robber at the movie theater.

"You'll never believe what happened on my date with Nick last night," Jessica opened, itching to recount the entire story.

"Let's see." Elizabeth pretended to think. "I know! He kissed you."

"Duh," Jessica said impatiently, throwing a pillow at her sister. "You could at least try to guess something unusual."

"You bought the tickets?" Elizabeth ventured, the corners of her mouth twitching with a barely suppressed smile.

Jessica was starting to wonder if Elizabeth was paying her back for the early wake-up call.

"No," Jessica told her twin importantly. "A guy tried to hold up the cashier with a gun and Nick stopped him single-handedly."

"You're kidding!" Elizabeth gasped, clearly stunned.

That's more like it, Jessica noted with satisfaction. "You should have seen him, Liz," she enthused. Jessica closed her eyes, trying to recapture the whole event herself. "Nick was absolutely amazing."

"Was anyone hurt?"

Jessica sighed. As usual, Elizabeth was getting bogged down in minor details.

"Of course not. I just told you—Nick was a total hero."

"Did the police come?" Elizabeth asked next.

"Of course! *Who cares?* I'm talking about Nick." It was so frustrating the way Elizabeth couldn't stick to a single subject. Sometimes Jessica wondered how her sister ever got all those news stories written for the campus television station.

"So Nick was pretty spectacular?"

Finally! "He was unbelievable," Jessica gushed.

"My night was pretty unbelievable too," Elizabeth said, kicking off her blanket and getting out of bed. "Mr. Conroy took Tom and me to Andre's."

"Get out of town!" Jessica exclaimed, shocked into momentarily forgetting Nick. "He did not!"

"No, really." Elizabeth nonchalantly opened the ridiculous little cupboard that the university called a closet and started looking for an outfit. "You'd love it there, Jess."

For a full minute Jessica was torn. On the one hand, it was so like Elizabeth to one-up her without even trying, but on the other hand, Jessica was dying to hear about Andre's. In the end curiosity won out.

"So was it as fabulous as everybody says?" she asked.

"More so," Elizabeth answered, pulling an old button-down blouse and a white cardigan off their hangers and lying them out on her bed. Jessica made a face automatically, then looked down at her own stylish hip huggers and red crop top with satisfaction.

"What did you wear?" Jessica asked.

"As a matter of fact," Elizabeth said with a smile, "your strapless black dress."

"*My* dress?" Jessica squeaked, outraged.

"Turnabout is fair play." Elizabeth pushed her feet into fuzzy pink slippers and began assembling her shower bag for the bathroom.

"But I only borrow your clothes when it's absolutely necessary," Jessica protested. *Like when I need someone to think I'm you,* she added silently. Elizabeth always got really tweaked when she did that.

"It *was* necessary, Jess," Elizabeth said. "You should see that place. They have antique chandeliers everywhere, and real china and crystal on the tables. And the silverware is *silver*ware."

"Do the waiters really wear tuxedos?" Jessica asked, sparking to her sister's enthusiasm in spite of her irritation about the dress.

"The *dishwashers* wear tuxedos. And the women . . . well, you've never seen so many diamonds."

It seemed to Jessica that a cloud passed over her sister's face at the mention of diamonds—not that Jessica could imagine why. When she got older, she planned to have loads of them.

"It sounds heavenly," Jessica said dreamily,

imagining herself at Andre's on a date with Nick. "Mr. Conroy must have major bucks."

Elizabeth quickly finished stuffing her shower bag and turned her back to the room to brush out her hair. Jessica could still see her sister's face reflected in the mirror, though. Oddly enough, it wasn't the happy, glowing face of a girl who'd just scored a major social coup. If anything, Elizabeth looked worried. *Leave it to Liz.* Jessica sighed to herself. "What's the matter?" she asked resignedly.

"Nothing!" Elizabeth said, brushing her hair harder. "Why do you think something's wrong?"

"It's all over your face, Liz. What happened? Did you use the wrong fork or something?"

Elizabeth didn't even smile. "Sorry to disappoint you, Jessica," she responded primly. "It was a perfect evening."

Jessica shrugged. "If you say so. Anyway, I've got to go." She got up and began rummaging under her bed for her book bag. She knew it had to be under there somewhere—unless maybe it was under the pile of laundry in the corner. One of these days she'd have to wash some clothes.

"Where are you going?" Elizabeth asked, turning from the mirror to face her. "It's only seven-thirty!"

Jessica located the book bag at last and dumped its contents out on top of her unmade bed. "Theta house meeting," she said, her voice assuming a grim tone. "We're voting on whether or not to admit Celine Boudreaux."

"You need to vote?" Elizabeth exclaimed, clearly appalled. "Isn't it obvious?"

"Don't worry," Jessica said, setting her jaw. "There's no way she's getting in."

"May I have everyone's attention, please?" the Theta president, Magda Helperin, called from the polished oak podium at the front of the meeting room. Seated next to Magda, facing the rest of the sorority sisters, was Alison Quinn, and seated next to Alison was Celine. "Please, everyone. Come to order."

Celine surveyed the Thetas from her vantage point in the front of the room, trying to gauge her chances of being voted into the sorority. Even though Alison kept assuring her it was practically a done deal, the sad truth was that Alison wasn't that smart. Incredibly useful, but not particularly smart. Celine watched impatiently as the room filled, making sure to smile extra sweetly at anyone who looked her way.

"I'm so nervous," she whispered to Alison, playing for sympathy. "I'll just die if I don't get in."

Alison reached over and squeezed Celine's hand. "Don't you worry," she whispered, patting the papers in her lap with a confident smile. "My speech is going to knock them dead."

The hubbub in the room gradually died down as the Thetas took their seats, and Magda resumed speaking. "As you know, we are holding this special house meeting today to vote on the question of admitting Celine Boudreaux into Theta Alpha Theta. A vote like this—for a person who has neither rushed nor pledged—is extremely unusual and must be considered carefully. However, in light of Celine's recent contributions to our house . . ."

Celine tuned out Magda's voice as she droned on and on, repeating what everyone there already knew. Instead Celine took the opportunity to study the faces of the girls before her, searching for clues as to how they would vote. It was early in the morning, and most of the Thetas still looked half asleep, but many of them smiled encouragingly as their eyes met hers. Celine felt her hopes start to rise as she humbly returned each smile. Alison was right—things did look pretty promising.

Then Celine's eyes met Jessica Wakefield's and her optimism faltered. Jessica was sitting in the back with her group of cronies—Lila Fowler, Isabella Ricci, Denise Waters, and that Alex girl—staring daggers at Celine. *I just have to keep my head,* Celine told herself, taking a deep breath. *That self-righteous little shrew isn't going to make this easy, but I have Alison on my side.* Celine turned her attention back toward Alison, buttering her up with her sweetest, most helpless smile.

"Before we put this to a vote," Magda's voice broke through into Celine's consciousness, "does anyone wish to address the group?"

"I do!" Jessica Wakefield shouted, jumping to

her feet in an unladylike hurry. "I *definitely* do."

"Go ahead, Jessica." Magda took a seat on the other side of the podium as Jessica worked her way to the front of the room.

"Celine Boudreaux does not deserve to be a Theta," Jessica began abruptly, thumping the podium for emphasis. "She's dangerous, vindictive, and probably even crazy. She and her friend William White actually tried to *kill* fellow SVU students, and there's no reason to believe that she won't do it again. As a matter of fact, when Celine roomed with my sister, Elizabeth . . ."

Celine watched Jessica speak without really hearing what she was saying. These Wakefields were so predictable—always acting as if they had the high moral ground when all they really wanted was to get their own way. It would have been comical if it wasn't so inconvenient. Celine had to admit, though—this wilder version of her ex-roommate, Princess Elizabeth, had a certain flair.

"And *finally,*" Jessica concluded passionately, coming to the end of her speech, "admitting Celine into the Thetas would jeopardize the sorority's position as the most elite house on campus. No other sorority at SVU would even look at her. Therefore, I hope you'll all agree *not* to vote her in."

"Thank you, Jessica," Magda said, regaining the podium. "Your remarks will be considered."

Jessica hesitated at the front of the room just

long enough to direct one last, poisonous look at Celine before she headed back to her seat.

"We will take Jessica's speech to be the argument *against* admitting Celine," Magda continued calmly. "Would anyone like to speak on Celine's behalf?"

"I would, Madame President," Alison said, rising gracefully.

"All right, Alison," Magda agreed, yielding the podium once more.

Celine was gratified to see how dignified Alison appeared as she took her place behind the podium and prepared to speak. Not only was she observing every propriety of house procedure, Alison had dressed for business in a tailored navy dress with a single strand of pearls. It made for an unavoidable and favorable comparison with Jessica, who had addressed her sisters wearing the top half of a red shirt and white bell-bottoms.

"Everyone in this house knows where Jessica Wakefield stands with regard to Celine," Alison began, her tone friendly and reasonable. "But does everyone here realize that Jessica doesn't know Celine?"

A quick, confused murmur ran through the audience.

"It's true," Alison said. "Jessica's opinions of Celine are all taken from chance encounters and secondhand gossip."

Jessica almost choked on her own tongue at

that, and Celine could barely keep the smile off her face as she pretended to hang on Alison's every word.

"I *know* Celine," Alison continued calmly. "I can honestly tell you that she's a wonderful, warm, *caring* person. And as far as Jessica's assertion that Celine doesn't deserve to be a Theta is concerned, she couldn't be more wrong. For what is a Theta? A Theta is a leader, a woman committed to excellence in all endeavors."

What followed was some of the most skillful propaganda Celine had ever heard. Alison spread on the verbal syrup with a trowel, and Celine watched with satisfaction as the Thetas licked up every drop. *Maybe I underestimated old Alison,* Celine allowed to herself, smiling, as Alison's speech finally came to its climax.

"For who among us can say that she's never made a mistake?" Alison asked, her voice quivering with emotion. "Who among us has never been forgiven? Yet this is what Jessica Wakefield would have us do—judge another and withhold forgiveness. Yes, Celine Boudreaux has made mistakes—she's the first to admit it. But she deserves another chance! We have it in our hands today to extend the forgiveness that would set Celine on a new and better road. We have it in our hearts today to welcome her into our midst and embrace her as one of us. Celine Boudreaux *must* become a Theta—not only because she deserves it but also because a *true* Theta could never vote any other way."

The conclusion of Alison's speech was met by thunderous noise as first one, then many of the sorority sisters stood, applauding wildly.

Oh, brother, Celine thought, dabbing at her eyes with a handkerchief. *What a brilliant piece of drivel.*

"Order!" Magda cried as Alison slipped triumphantly back into the chair next to Celine. "We'll vote now."

"All in favor of admitting Celine Boudreaux into Theta Alpha Theta, please stand and say 'aye.'"

"Aye!" was the immediate and overwhelming response. For as far as Celine could see, her new sorority sisters were standing, smiling at her with tear-filled eyes.

"Those opposed?" Magda asked.

"Nay!" came the vehement reply from the back of the room—Jessica Wakefield and her gang of four.

"Very well, then," Magda said, turning to Celine and smiling. "Congratulations, Celine, and welcome. You are hereby declared a sister of Theta Alpha Theta."

Alison rose to her feet immediately, applauding with three fingers of her right hand against the palm of her left. "Speech!" she cried, urging Celine to stand beside her.

"I couldn't," Celine demurred, rising and smoothing the skirt of her old-fashioned white cotton dress. "Y'all have been so nice to me. I . . . I just don't know what to say."

"Speech!" Some of the other Thetas took up the cry, smiling at Celine encouragingly.

"Well, if y'all insist," Celine said modestly, moving toward the podium.

A sudden motion at the back of the room caught Celine's attention. Jessica and her friends were standing to walk out, and to Celine's unmitigated delight, Jessica looked positively furious.

"Let me just start by thanking everyone so much for believing in me," Celine drawled, looking directly at Jessica and smiling triumphantly.

Jessica tossed her blond hair and stalked out the meeting-room door in a rage.

Alex made her way slowly across the SVU campus, her stomach churning. Although a couple of hours had passed since the house meeting, somehow her mind still refused to accept the fact that Celine Boudreaux had actually been voted into the Thetas. It wasn't fair and, more than that, it wasn't right. How could a dangerous sleaze like Celine just waltz right into the most exclusive sorority on campus for the price of a few new furnishings? It made Alex sick to think about it, especially when she remembered how thrilled and proud she herself had been when the Thetas had selected her for membership. It was all cheapened now, tarnished by the sorority's acceptance of Celine.

I need a drink, Alex thought before she could stop herself. Nothing in her life was going right anyway.

First the breakup with Noah and now this . . . what difference would it make if she turned around and headed for the nearest liquor store? Alex's steps faltered, then stopped.

"No!" Alex said out loud, forcing her feet in the right direction again. "You are *not* going to do that."

Drinking wouldn't solve anything—it would just make things worse. If she hadn't learned that by now, her case was hopeless.

I'll go to the hot line, she decided suddenly. *That will help take my mind off it.*

Alex hurried to the hot-line offices and pushed eagerly through the entrance door. "Hi, Doug," she called, crossing to the phone room. Then, before Doug could even reply, "How about letting me take some calls today?"

"I don't know if that's such a good idea," Doug said slowly, turning to face her and fidgeting with his operator's headset. "You've only monitored calls for a few hours. Are you sure you're ready to take one yourself?"

"I know I am." Alex looked around the phone room of the tiny hot-line office with determination. Since it was Monday and classes were in session, the phones were slow, and Doug was the only operator working. It was the perfect opportunity for her to get her feet wet.

Doug still hesitated.

"You can shadow my call on the loudspeaker

and step in any time," Alex pointed out reasonably.

"Well, all right," Doug said, rising from his chair and removing his headset. "Have a seat."

He gestured Alex into the folding metal chair he'd just vacated and settled the headphones down over her thick auburn waves. "How does that feel?"

"OK," she answered, adjusting the microphone to a spot in front of her mouth. She twisted in her chair to face him. "How do I look?"

Doug laughed. "Stunning."

Alex grinned sheepishly as she realized the full idiocy of her question. She hadn't asked out of vanity; she'd only wanted to be reassured that she looked professional, capable. But of course no one was ever going to *see* her—that was the whole idea behind an anonymous hot line.

"OK. We've got one," Doug said suddenly.

Alex spun back around in her chair to see a light blinking on the switchboard. She flipped the switch for the loudspeaker and then, with a quick intake of breath, connected the call. "SVU Substance Abuse Hot Line," she said with crisp efficiency. "How can I help you?"

There was the usual hesitation on the other end before the caller finally spoke. "I . . . I shouldn't have called," a girl's voice said. "Never mind."

"No, wait!" Alex blurted before the caller could hang up. Her voice had sounded too cold, too clinical when she'd answered the line, Alex realized. She wanted to be professional, but she could still be warm. "I'd really like to help you with anything I can," she told the girl sincerely.

Doug nodded approval and encouragement.

"I don't think anyone can *help* me," the caller said after a pause. "I just kind of wanted someone to talk to."

"You can talk to me," Alex assured her. "I can talk as long as you want." That wasn't exactly true—she had another class in an hour—but she'd *make* it true if she had to.

"I . . . I had a big fight with my best friend yesterday," the girl on the phone said at last. "It was really awful."

There was another long pause. "Uh-huh," Alex prompted.

"I guess maybe I shouldn't even call her my best friend anymore," the caller continued. "I don't know. Nothing's been the same between us since we came to college. It seems like we barely even know each other now."

Alex winced involuntarily, thinking of Elizabeth Wakefield. Nothing between *them* had been the same since they'd come to college either, and it probably never would be again. Ever since they'd graduated from high school their lives had moved in opposite directions, the distance between them crystallized by Alex's brief, doomed fling with Todd Wilkins.

"Sometimes that happens," Alex told the caller, "but it doesn't mean you don't still care about each other."

The girl drew in a shuddering breath. "I doubt she's going to care about me when she finds out what I did with her boyfriend last night. But she makes me so mad! Like she thinks she's so much better than everyone else. And it's not just me, you know. Jeff—that's her boyfriend—is fighting with her too. So yesterday . . . I don't know—maybe I was trying to get her back. Maybe we both were."

It was a like a bad déjà vu, Alex realized, fighting to stay calm. "You and Jeff . . ." She let the question trail off.

"Yeah," the girl confirmed. "Afraid so. I was drunk and so was he and it just kind of happened. We've been drinking together a lot lately. I think it was the alcohol that made us do it."

"Don't you think maybe *people* make things happen?" Alex asked.

"What do you mean?"

"Like whatever happened between you and Jeff. Is it possible that alcohol only gave you both an excuse to do what you wanted to do anyway?"

"I don't think I *wanted* to sleep with my best friend's boyfriend!" the caller protested hotly.

"I didn't say you did," Alex replied, keeping her voice pleasant. "But you did say you were mad at her and wanted to get her back. Do you and Jeff really have feelings for each other, or is it possible you only did this to hurt your friend?"

For a minute all Alex could hear was breathing.

She's not going to answer me—I've blown it, she worried, too nervous to look at Doug.

"I don't know," the caller said at last. "Maybe."

"I know what you're going through," Alex assured her sympathetically. "I do. But at some point you're going to have to stop—stop drinking, stop hurting your friends, and stop hurting yourself. It's easy to say alcohol made you do something, but what made you do the alcohol?"

"I guess," the girl agreed.

"If you *want* to stop, you can," Alex encouraged her. "I'm going to give you phone numbers for some places that can help you. And you can always call back here. Anytime."

Alex finished giving her caller the help-line numbers, then disconnected the line with a shaking hand. It had been harder than she'd thought it would be, but she felt as if she'd done well.

"Excellent!" Doug congratulated her as soon as the light blinked out. "Way to go!"

"I'm afraid that was kind of an easy call for me," Alex told him, trying to smile and failing. "You could say I've been there, done that."

It was still painful to remember those old times, the times before Noah had come into her life. *If only he'd been a little more sensitive,* Alex thought, wishing she could erase that stupid fight from their lives and put things back the way they'd been.

"Uh, Alex?" a familiar voice said from the doorway. "Can I talk to you a minute?"

"Noah!" Alex leaped up from her chair in surprise. "What are you doing here?"

"I went by your room and Trina told me you might be here," Noah explained, looking uncomfortable but incredibly handsome at the same time. "Could we talk for a minute . . . alone?"

"I've got a test I wouldn't mind studying for," Doug offered immediately. "If you could cover the phones for the next few minutes until Richard gets here, Alex . . ."

"Sure, Doug," Alex agreed gratefully. "Thanks."

In two steps Doug was out of the tiny phone room and in another two he was out the door.

Noah hesitated only a moment. "Alex, I'm so sorry."

She nodded. "So am I," she said coolly. "I thought you had a little more faith in me, Noah."

"I do!" he said, reaching for her hands, but she put them quickly behind her, out of reach.

"You sure have a funny way of showing it. You thought I was going to start drinking again," she accused.

Noah stepped back, rebuffed. "You said you wanted to," he reminded her in a low voice.

"That's right. I said I *wanted* to. I *always* want to, but I'm not doing it, am I?"

"No. I'm so sorry."

"Can't you understand that this isn't the type of problem that goes away overnight? I'm not just whining, Noah—I struggle with this every day."

"I didn't realize—" he began unhappily.

"I know you don't realize!" Alex exploded, her voice shaking with emotion. "That's the whole problem. And I keep trying to tell you, but you never listen."

"I listen," Noah protested. "I listen to everything you say."

"Then why doesn't any of it sink in? I don't need clichés and platitudes, Noah. I need your *help.*"

For a long moment Noah was silent, his deep-set brown eyes searching hers. At last he spoke. "How can I help you?" he asked quietly.

"Well, you can believe in me, for one thing," Alex told him, softening a little. "And that doesn't mean telling me that I'm smart and all my problems are in my head—it means really being there for me when things get rough."

Noah nodded, then held out his arms to her. "I can do that," he said.

He looked so sincere and so contrite that Alex hesitated only a second before she threw herself into his embrace. "Oh, Noah," she said, wrapping her arms around him.

"I never meant to make you feel bad about yourself," Noah whispered into her hair.

"You didn't!" Alex assured him. "You don't." She tilted her face up to his and he kissed her. "I missed you so much," she admitted.

Noah smiled, pushing his shaggy blond hair back out of his eyes. "I missed you more," he teased.

He looked around the tiny phone room, and Alex wondered if he was remembering his own days as an operator on the main campus hot line. He'd gone by the alias of T-Squared, and when Alex had called him, she'd said her name was Enid, thinking no one would know it was her. He'd helped her so much back then.

"It's not very glamorous," she said apologetically, gesturing at her operator's station. "Not like the main hot line."

"I think it's great," Noah said, pulling her back into his embrace. "I'm proud of you."

Alex could feel her throat getting tight. In another minute she'd be crying. "I love you, T-Squared," she whispered, hiding her face against his neck.

"I love you, Enid."

"Nina! Nina, wait up!"

Nina turned in the middle of the crowded quad and seemed surprised to see Elizabeth running in her direction.

"Hi," she said as Elizabeth finally reached her. "What's up? Don't you have English now?"

"Yeah, but I'm not going," Elizabeth answered, struggling to catch her breath. "I'm way ahead in that class and I've got to talk to you."

Nina looked concerned. "What's the matter?"

"It's nothing major," Elizabeth said, reluctant to make a big deal out of a little misunderstanding. But was it a misunderstanding? Last night, after an incredible meal and two glasses of champagne, she'd managed to convince herself that it was. This morning she wasn't so sure. "Could we take a walk somewhere?" she asked Nina. "Maybe out by the playing fields?"

"Sure." Nina pulled the second strap of her purple backpack up onto her shoulder and shrugged her load of books into place. "Let's go."

As the two girls wandered across the crowded campus Elizabeth started wondering once again if she was being silly. She was probably totally overreacting. She ought to be in English class, not wasting Nina's time dragging her all over campus. But even as she thought it, Elizabeth knew she wouldn't have heard a word the professor said. She turned her head to look at Nina, who smiled at her encouragingly.

"Mr. Conroy took Tom and me to Andre's last night," Elizabeth began, planning to work her way around to the real subject gradually.

Nina's eyebrows shot up. She was clearly impressed, even though she was trying not to show it. "Fancy," she said.

"Very," Elizabeth agreed, but it no longer gave her any kind of thrill.

"You didn't like it?" Nina asked.

Elizabeth realized she should have known Nina would sense her lack of enthusiasm immediately. "It's not that—"

"Don't tell me something went wrong between Tom and Mr. Conroy!" Nina interrupted loudly.

"No, nothing like that," Elizabeth assured her. "In fact, I've never seen Tom so happy."

"Then what's the problem?" Nina's face was puzzled.

Elizabeth winced, but she knew she was going to have to say it sooner or later. "It's Mr. Conroy." Her voice came out so low, she could barely hear it. "I think he likes me."

"What?" Nina said, clearly not sure she'd heard correctly. "Of *course* he likes you. After everything you did to help him . . ."

"No, Nina. I think he *likes* me."

"He *what?* Oh, gross!"

"No kidding," Elizabeth said glumly. They reached the end of the quad and headed down a concrete walkway in the direction of the athletics fields. The crush of students was less dense there and Elizabeth raised her voice a little. "I mean, how could he do this to Tom?"

"Are you sure about this? What did he say to you?" Nina asked, her brown eyes locked intently on Elizabeth's blue-green ones. "What did he do?"

"I don't know. Nothing really overt. He held my hand and said a bunch of stuff about how pretty I was and would I consider going out with an old guy like him. It was so embarrassing."

"He asked you out?" Nina looked shocked.

"Not exactly," Elizabeth admitted. "But I'm

pretty sure that's what he was getting at. Oh, Nina, what am I going to do?"

"I don't know," Nina said slowly. "What does Tom think?"

Elizabeth's eyes dropped to the sidewalk, where her feet paced along confidently, as if they belonged to someone else. "He doesn't know yet. He was in the bathroom when it happened."

"Oh, wow. This gets uglier and uglier."

The two girls walked in silence a few minutes, pondering the situation. The playing fields came into sight, and Elizabeth turned mechanically toward some folding metal bleachers at the edge of the nearest field. A group of guys was playing touch football one field over, but no one was on the first field and the bleachers were completely empty. Elizabeth climbed straight to the top row of seats, Nina right behind her, before she turned and sat down.

"I think I should tell Tom what happened," Elizabeth said uncertainly. "But what if I'm wrong?"

"Wrong?" Nina repeated, looking confused. "Do you think there's any chance of that?"

"I don't know," Elizabeth admitted. How was it possible to feel so great one day and so miserable the next? "I don't think so, but I'm not positive either. I mean, Mr. Conroy came on really strong while Tom was in the bathroom, and then he dropped it completely. Maybe I imagined the whole thing."

Nina looked worried. "If you're not one hundred percent sure—"

"I know," Elizabeth interrupted unhappily.

"You've got to think about what it would do to Tom," Nina cautioned.

"It would kill him."

Tom was a sweet, intelligent, levelheaded guy—except when he was jealous, and then all bets were off. Elizabeth shuddered at the awful mental picture of telling Tom that his wonderful new father was hitting on her. "I can't do it," she whispered. Not if she wasn't certain. And probably not even if she was.

Nina looked relieved. "I think you're making the right decision," she said, patting Elizabeth on the arm. "You know I'd back you up either way, but this is a bad time to make a big stink. *Especially* if there's any possibility of a misunderstanding."

"I know." Elizabeth groaned, dropping her head into her hands. "And it was probably nothing. I bet I totally misread the entire situation."

So then why did she feel so creeped out?

A raucous cheer from the players on the nearby football field caught the girls' attention. One side had just scored a touchdown and was rubbing the other side's nose in it. A few spectators, mostly girlfriends, joined in the noise. Elizabeth and Nina watched in silence for a while as the hotly contested intramural match raged on.

"Look at that strange guy on the phone over

there," Nina said suddenly, pointing. "Do you think he even knows he's in the middle of a football game?"

Elizabeth followed Nina's finger. A tall, brown-haired guy stood just off the sidelines. He didn't seem the slightest bit concerned about bodily harm as he spoke into a cell phone, his back toward the bleachers.

"Hey, don't we know him?" Nina added, sitting up taller and straining for a better view. "He seems familiar."

"I don't think so," Elizabeth began, but then stopped. Wait a minute—wasn't that Jessica's new boyfriend, Nick? Elizabeth had only met him once, at Tom's party, but she was pretty sure it was him. *Why is he talking on a phone in the middle of the athletics fields?* she wondered. Elizabeth shook her head, resigned to the idea that she'd probably never find out. Still, it was undeniably strange behavior.

Jessica and her guys, Elizabeth thought, bracing for what looked like another one of her sister's romantic disasters. *She sure can pick 'em.*

Celine pushed her grocery cart distractedly down the aisle, looking for something easy to make for lunch. *And cheap!* she reminded herself, averting her gaze from the seafood counter. She was dangerously low on cash.

It's hateful of Granny to be so stingy, she thought for the thousandth time as her eyes roamed the culinary possibilities. Jordan was already so out of his league even dating her that Celine knew he'd be happy with a bowl of cold cereal, but she needed to maintain the illusion of being interested in him—at least until she got what she wanted.

"And I *always* get what I want," she muttered under her breath, turning her cart up the pasta aisle. After all, hadn't she just been voted into the Thetas? If her grandmother had simply coughed up a few lousy bucks, Celine could be polishing her nails right now and planning her next social triumph. Instead she was preparing to entertain a social loser.

She tossed some interesting-shaped pasta into her cart and followed it up with a small glass jar of tomato sauce. She knew from unfortunate personal experience that with a little added hamburger and mushroom, the average guy couldn't tell bottled sauce from homemade. Of course Italian sausage was good too, but Celine didn't have money for sausage. *He can eat French bread instead and like it!* she thought fiercely.

Pulling her cart over to the side of the aisle, Celine paused to open her purse and count her money again. It was humiliating that any Boudreaux—especially herself—should be so short of cash, and Celine glanced self-consciously around to make sure no one was watching. Her last coin slipped through her fingers as Celine finished counting. She had enough to pay for the groceries, but this little lunch party was going to clean her out. There was no way around it—she had to put her moneymaking plan into action immediately.

Celine closed her eyes for a second, picturing Jordan and mentally running over their upcoming lunch date. She knew she looked hot in the tight red minidress she'd changed into after the Theta meeting—her ability to vamp the guy wasn't even an issue—but she still had to play things just right. If Jordan got scared and talked to someone . . . her blue eyes flew open, and she took a few deep breaths to calm her nerves.

As annoying as it was, she needed Jordan. In fact, he was the key to her entire get-rich-quick scheme. Without Jordan in the middle to take the heat, her plan was way too dangerous. *It's probably too dangerous anyway,* Celine thought, her pulse a sickening thud. But what choice did she have? It was the only way she could think of to raise the money she needed—the money she'd promised the Thetas for their new parlor. Her mission for this afternoon was to somehow convince Jordan to do her dirty work for her.

Celine looked down at the groceries in her cart and wondered what she'd be eating when they were gone. "This guy better not be a dud," she said out loud as she headed for the register.

Chapter Six

"Uh . . . everything tasted great, Celine," Jordan said, shifting awkwardly in his seat. "Thanks."

"Why, you're very welcome." Celine made sure she bent over at just the right angle to give Jordan a good peek down the front of her tight red dress as she reached to clear his plate from the table. His pale blue eyes widened noticeably, then quickly looked away. She knew she'd been successful.

Celine stood holding their dirty lunch plates, watching critically as her victim squirmed in his hard dinette chair. Jordan's usually pale, freckled cheeks were flushed a brilliant shade of pink, and he wouldn't meet her gaze. *This boy has absolutely no control over his body language,* Celine noted with disgust, hoping it wouldn't turn out to be a problem later. Quickly she gathered up the rest of the dishes and carried them over to the sink, where she dropped them into some soapy water. She'd take care of them later—right now she had more important things to do.

"Come on over here and relax, sugar," she invited, moving from the kitchen into the living room and dropping gracefully onto her tacky rented sofa. Everything was so cramped in her pitiful one-bedroom apartment—only a few steps in any direction would take you to another room. Celine hated living in such a dive, and the fact that it was off campus just made it that much worse. Living in the dorms had been crowded too, but at least no one had expected anything better there. After all, Celine couldn't be held responsible for the university's lack of taste.

Unfortunately living in the dorms wasn't an option for Celine anymore—not since she'd gotten involved with William White's insane plan to kill her ex-roommate, Elizabeth. The very thought of Elizabeth made Celine wince with dislike, but Elizabeth's twin sister, Jessica, was turning out to be every bit as annoying. How dare she oppose Celine's entrance into the Thetas?

"I wish I'd never even *heard* the name Wakefield," Celine muttered, not realizing she was talking out loud.

"What?" Jordan asked. He was standing up now, but he still hadn't moved from his spot by the dinette. The guy was a total innocent—Celine felt as if she were baby-sitting.

"I said come and sit here with me, Jordan." She patted the sofa cushion next to hers and smiled as invitingly as she could. "Tell me all about yourself."

Jordan crossed the room toward Celine, stopping uncertainly just as he got to the couch. Then, with an obvious intake of breath, he rushed the last two steps to her side and practically dove onto the sofa. The guy was about as smooth as steel wool.

"That's better," Celine purred, snuggling up against him, both her tiny hands on his left arm. "So what are you majoring in, Jordan, darling?" Her accent dripped sugar.

Jordan hesitated, clearly nervous. All through lunch Celine had barely gotten two complete words out of him. The fact that he was shy was useful, but things would be easier if he were a little less shy with *her*.

"Celine," he said suddenly, turning to look at her. "Why are you being so nice to me?"

Celine raised an eyebrow. "Why, whatever do you mean, sugar?"

Jordan was blushing furiously, but he continued anyway. "I mean, you're beautiful. And I'm just a geeky little freshman. What could you possibly see in me?"

There went that intelligent streak again. Celine sighed, then pushed her bottom lip forward in a slight pout and widened her baby blue eyes. "Is that what you think of me?" she asked in a wounded tone. "That all I care about is how people look?" She dropped his arm and moved an inch away.

"No!" Jordan exclaimed, clearly rattled. "I mean . . . it's just that . . . well . . . well, don't you?"

Celine retreated another calculated inch. "Now isn't that just like a man? Some poor girl takes a chance to try to get to know him, and he's all the time thinking the worst of her." She ran her eyes sadly down his body. "I really thought you were different, Jordan."

"You did? I mean, I am!" He looked so distraught that Celine could barely keep from laughing out loud.

"I suppose that's the only reason you went out with *me,*" she continued, ignoring his interruption. "Because of how I *look.*"

"That's not true," Jordan protested. "I wanted to get to know you too."

"Really?" Celine inched back over on the couch and treated him to her biggest, most brilliant smile. "You're not just saying that?"

"Really," he assured her. "I mean, of course you're beautiful—incredibly so—but I wanted to know you as a person too."

Celine dropped her eyes modestly. She'd always wished she could blush at will, the way some of the girls at her cotillion could, but she had to settle for batting her lashes a little instead.

"That's so nice," she murmured, hoping to convey the impression that she was overcome by his compliments. "I knew the second I saw you that you'd be nice."

"Oh. Well . . ." Jordan looked pleased but also completely nonplussed. She could tell he had no clue what to do next.

"Personally, I haven't declared a major yet," Celine continued, hoping to start a conversation Jordan could follow. "A lot of my sisters in the Thetas, well, it seems like they were just *born* knowing what they wanted to be when they grew up. But not me. My granny always said that a good girl only cared about one degree—her MRS."

"That's so sexist!" Jordan gasped, clearly sincere. "Women are just as smart as men."

He's kind of sweet, Celine thought, favoring him with a rare genuine smile. *Even if he wouldn't be worth my time in any other situation.* "Do you really think so?" she asked breathlessly, taking his arm again.

"Sure. There are lots of girls in my engineering classes, and they're every bit as smart as the guys. That's what I'm going to major in, I think—engineering."

"Engineering!" Celine was an expert at sounding impressed by the trivial revelations of men, and her talent didn't fail her this time.

Jordan sat up straighter on the sofa and actually ventured another look at her face.

"You must be a genius," she added, reaching up and removing his baseball cap.

He'd been gradually gaining confidence over the previous few minutes, but the intimate way Celine took his hat seemed to undo Jordan completely. He began sputtering again and squirming self-consciously.

"Don't talk, sugar," she said, bringing her lips to his. Please *don't talk,* she thought.

His lips were soft for a man's—very soft. They reminded her of William's. Celine's eyes flew open, only to stare directly into Jordan's pale ice blue ones. *Yes,* she thought, slowly closing her eyes again. The comparison with William White wasn't unwelcome—imagining Jordan was William would help Celine do whatever intimate things she must to convince Jordan to help her. Her mouth moved on his, teasing, exploring. Gradually he relaxed and began returning her kisses.

Celine put her arms around him, pulling herself up onto his lap. The denim of his still-new jeans felt rough against the backs of her bare thighs, which her minidress didn't cover. She ran her hands slowly through his cropped white blond hair and then down his back, feeling his underdeveloped muscles jump nervously through the fabric of his gray polo shirt.

"Why, you're wound up tighter than a cat at a dog show," she murmured against his lips, putting her hands to work while her lips moved to explore his neck.

It wasn't the way Celine would have *chosen* to spend a half hour, but it wasn't completely horrible. She was lucky, really. A lot of guys would have wanted more from her. But by the end of thirty minutes of only basic making out, Jordan was putty in her hands. It was time to get serious.

"I know what *you're* up to," Celine said flirtatiously, climbing out of his lap. "You're trying to make me miss my afternoon class."

Jordan looked indescribably pleased with himself, as if he were actually capable of making that happen. "I didn't know you had a class, Celine," he said. "But anyway, *I've* already missed two."

Good. Then he was as under her spell as she'd thought. "For little old me?" she teased. "I'm flattered."

He laughed ruefully. "You *should* be. One of them was chemistry and we had a quiz today."

"You missed a quiz!" He really *was* all hers.

"Yeah, but don't worry," he said, misreading her totally. "We get to throw out our lowest quiz score, so I can make it up by doing well on all the others."

"In that case," Celine said, walking toward the kitchen, "how about staying for dessert?" She paused at the refrigerator and looked back over her shoulder at him.

"I thought we already *had* dessert," Jordan joked awkwardly, blushing.

Celine smiled at his attempt at humor and pulled a half empty pint of raspberry sherbet out of the freezer. She was pretty sure Jordan had never been kissed the way she'd just kissed him. At first he'd barely responded—it was like kissing Jell-O. Then he'd started to get into it, but awkwardly, uncertainly. It wasn't until just before they'd stopped that he'd seemed to really get the hang of it.

The next girl to come his way owes me a big thank-you, Celine thought, dropping round scoops of sherbet into glass dessert dishes. Not that she didn't plan to get paid back *well* before that unlikely event occurred.

"Here you go, sugar," she said, coming back to the couch with two dishes of sherbet and some long dessert spoons. She handed Jordan his, then sat on the coffee table facing him. "I hope you like raspberry."

"Sure," he said, beginning to shovel down his little scoop too quickly. He was getting nervous again. If she didn't act fast, Celine realized, she'd have to start all over.

"Oooh, I just thought of something," she squealed, faking excited delight. "I want you to call this guy I know."

Jordan didn't look up from his disappearing sherbet. "Why?" he asked. "What guy?"

"His name is Nick Fox. Do you know him?"

Celine was relieved to see Jordan shake his head no. The chances of a loser like Jordan knowing someone like Nick were one in a million, of course, but she couldn't be too careful now that she was getting so close to the dangerous part of her plan.

Celine lifted her cordless phone off the coffee table and started dialing Nick's number. She'd memorized it as soon as he'd given it to her and burned the piece of paper it was written on—no sane person would keep something that incriminating lying around the house. She pressed the final number and extended the phone to Jordan. "When Nick answers," she said casually, "I want to play a little joke on him. You just ask him if he wants to buy a shipment."

Jordan's head jerked up from his dessert plate. "What kind of shipment?" he asked in a panicky voice. "Not drugs!"

Celine instantly hit the button to disconnect the call. Jordan's voice was so loud, the entire apartment complex had probably heard him! If Nick had answered during that . . . Celine's heart thudded erratically and her hands shook as she put the phone back down on the table. She felt as if she might be sick.

Taking a few deep, reassuring breaths, Celine

moved to regain control of the situation. "Drugs?" she repeated, laughing lightly. "My, my, Jordan. What an imagination you have!"

Jordan looked down at his dessert spoon and blushed. "I'm sorry," he said. "It's just kind of weird that you want me to call a total stranger for you. And then that stuff about a 'shipment.' You have to admit, Celine, *that* sounds a little suspicious."

Celine picked up her untouched sherbet and began eating it in minuscule bites, mainly for effect, while she stalled. She'd hoped that Jordan would do whatever she told him without asking questions, but unfortunately he was turning out to be a little smarter than she'd expected. Luckily she'd planned for that possibility too—her story was all ready.

"I can't believe you've never heard of Nick Fox," she told him, easing into the lie. "He *only* belongs to practically every environmental group on campus. He's always leading save-the-something-or-other demonstrations and speaking at the coffeehouse. You know, very sixties."

"Oh," Jordan said, knitting his pale brows. "Maybe I *have* heard of him."

Celine smiled encouragingly. *Liar,* she thought. "Well, I'll tell you the truth, sugar. Nick and I are old friends, but I can't call him myself this time." She took a deep breath and went on. "Now, Jordan, I don't want you thinking that I don't support animal rights, because I do. But there are limits to what I'm willing to do to help. I wouldn't, for instance, sacrifice a brother for the cause."

"What are you talking about?" Jordan looked completely confused, and that was good for Celine.

"My brother works for Hightower Pharmaceuticals," Celine replied. "Have you ever heard of them?"

Jordan shook his head. Of course he hadn't—Celine had made them up.

"Well, they're a very big company, and I'm afraid they're not a very nice one. My brother's spent the last six months gathering paperwork proving that Hightower does all kinds of laboratory testing on poor, defenseless animals. They're slime."

"Wow," Jordan breathed, buying every word.

"The kind of papers my brother has are exactly the type of thing that ol' Saint Nick just loves to get his hands on," Celine told him. "One look at these documents and Nick's backers'll be suing Hightower so fast, they won't know what hit them. They'll never torture animals again."

"But I still don't understand," Jordan protested. "Why don't you call Nick yourself?"

Celine let just a little irritation show. "*Because*, sugar, I already told you. If Nick knew I was involved, then he could trace the papers back to my brother. He could force my brother to testify in court. My brother would be fired, at best. At worst . . ." Celine faked a little shudder. "Who *knows* what those people would do to him?"

Jordan shuddered with her. "But Celine, if it's not safe—"

"It's perfectly safe for *you,* Jordan," she hurried to interrupt. "Nick doesn't know you from Adam. Besides, he's on our side."

"I don't know, Celine . . . ," Jordan began, looking doubtful.

Before he could go any further, Celine was back in his lap, pushing his empty sherbet plate onto the sofa cushions.

"Sometimes we have to do the things we *don't* like before we get to do the things we *do,*" she whispered, letting her lips graze against his ear. "Isn't that right, sugar?"

"What do you mean?" He seemed to be trying to resist, but he was already melting underneath her.

"My granny always says, 'Dinner before dessert,'" Celine said, nibbling his earlobe. "You like dessert pretty well, don't you, baby?"

Jordan moaned and drew her closer, planting his lips on hers. She let him kiss her a few minutes before she pulled away and picked up the telephone again. Dialing quickly, she handed the ringing phone to Jordan.

"Dinnertime," she said.

* * *

Jessica strode across the quad, her blue eyes stormy. It was an outrage that Celine had been admitted into the Thetas. No, worse than an outrage—a travesty! How could the most exclusive, most popular group of girls on campus have been so easily duped? Hadn't anyone listened to her at all?

This is all Alison's fault, Jessica thought, weaving her way impatiently through the slow-moving crowds of students. Alison Quinn had been out to get her for a long time. *And I'll bet she's just loving this,* Jessica told herself, disgusted. Well, the Thetas would find out what kind of person Celine was. Sooner or later Alison's little triumph would turn into everyone else's headache. And when that day came, Jessica planned to be the first one in line to say "I told you so." After all, hadn't she done her best to warn them?

Jessica smiled momentarily at the thought of her certain future vindication, but the satisfaction was fleeting. The future could be a long way away, and in the meantime Celine Boudreaux was a Theta. Every time Jessica thought about it, it ruined her day all over again. Even cutting her last class and hitting that fabulous sale at the mall with Lila hadn't cheered her up. Sure, she'd found a couple of great bargains—like the retro flower-print sundress she was wearing—but Lila had nagged her about picking up that stupid hat on Tuesday the entire time. And now, to make a bad day worse, Jessica was on her way back to her dorm room to do at least three weeks' worth of neglected homework assignments.

Oh no! Jessica thought, suddenly remembering. *I was supposed to pick up that reading assignment for American literature at the copy center.* The idea of walking all the way back to the copy center when she was already so close to her room in Dickenson Hall couldn't have been less appealing, and Jessica seriously considered blowing it off. She turned and looked back in the general direction of the copy center, mentally gauging the distance and begrudging the amount of time and effort the trip would take. There must be *someone* she knew that she could borrow the reading from. She was still trying to think of who when she spotted Nick.

He was sunning himself, shirtless, at the edge of the quad that was nearest the library. He looked too good to be real, and for a moment Jessica just stood there and admired him, forgetting everything else. The sloping grass Nick sat on in front of some of the oldest trees on campus was an ideal place to hang out and watch people go by, and Nick seemed to be simply relaxing and enjoying the show. But then, as Jessica watched, he pulled his cell phone from his shorts pocket and answered a call.

What a coincidence, Jessica thought, smiling and putting her feet into motion, *that's* exactly *the way I have to go to pick up that important assignment at the copy center.* Besides, if she snuck up behind him, she might be able to find out who he was always talking to on the phone. Changing her direction slightly, Jessica walked off the edge of the quad and continued along the back of the same strip of grass that Nick was sitting on. As she drew nearer, the big trees between her and Nick blocked her view of him, but she knew where he was. Moving as quickly and quietly as she could, Jessica crept up behind a tree and held her breath.

"What kind of shipment?" she heard Nick ask in a low, clipped voice. Jessica's eyes went wide. This was more like it! She snuck forward another tree.

"Documents?" he said.

She *knew* it! He *was* a spy. Jessica felt a thrill run all the way down to her bright red toenails. She could barely keep from bounding out of her hiding place.

"Who is this? Why are you calling me?" Nick demanded, then broke off, listening. Apparently the person on the other end of the phone was doing some fast talking, because Nick was silent for a long time. Jessica was tempted to peek around the tree to see if he was still there, but she couldn't risk letting him see her.

"I'll meet you," Nick said at last, "but let's get something straight. I'm not in this business to play games, all right? You want to sell me something, you say what. I don't want to hear any more cock-and-bull stories like that one." He sounded tough, and Jessica shivered with excitement.

"All right," Nick agreed, reacting to something the caller had said. "Tomorrow night, seven o'clock, behind the science building."

Jessica wasn't sure if the call was over or not, but she'd heard enough. There was going to be another pickup, and she was going to be there. She hurried away from Nick toward the library, then looped around and started walking up the concrete center of the quad, hoping Nick would still be sitting on the grass when she got there. He was, lost in thought, and Jessica decided to have some fun.

"Uh, excuse me," she said, approaching him as if he were a total stranger. "I was wondering if you could tell me where you got that shirt."

Nick looked down at his bare chest, clearly confused but wanting to play along. "Do you mean this one?" he asked at last, standing and removing an old T-shirt from his back shorts pocket, where it hung down like a wrinkled tail. He held it out to her.

"Yes, that one," Jessica confirmed, holding the shirt up in front of her and pretending to look it over. "It just looks so good *off*."

She'd have taken it further, but the expression on Nick's face was too much—she burst out giggling.

"You nut." He laughed, holding out his arms

for a hug. "What am I going to do with you?"

"Whatever you want," she teased huskily, throwing herself into his embrace. His skin was hot and smelled of soap and suntan lotion. She lifted her face to be kissed.

"Go out to dinner with me tonight," Nick urged when their lips finally parted.

"Well, I'll have to check my schedule," she fibbed, already planning her outfit. So much for American lit and all the rest of that ghastly homework. "Where are you taking me?"

"Wherever you want," Nick said. "Anywhere."

Jessica raised her eyebrows. "Anywhere?"

"You name it."

A slow, satisfied smile spread across Jessica's face. Unfortunately Elizabeth had worn her most formal dress the night before, but Jessica could always borrow something from one of her sorority sisters. *I'll get a dress from Lila,* Jessica decided, cranking up her smile another notch. *She'll have something I can wear to Andre's.*

Elizabeth put on mascara in front of her tiny dorm-room mirror, wishing all the while that she'd been smart enough to think of an excuse to miss the concert she was getting ready for. If only she'd had a test or something tomorrow! But in less than an hour the campus orchestra was giving its performance of Beethoven's Ninth, and unfortunately Tom and Mr. Conroy were expecting Elizabeth to go with them.

"At least this is the last time you'll have to see him for a while," Elizabeth told herself out loud, hoping to ease her own agitated mind. "Tomorrow he goes back to L.A."

She was talking about Mr. Conroy, of course. No matter how she tried to talk herself out of it, his behavior of the night before still gave her the creeps. Elizabeth finished up her eye makeup and started looking for something to wear. Since the concert was to be held outside, in the open-air amphitheater, she needed to dress warmly as well as nicely. After lengthy consideration Elizabeth decided on some brown dress pants, a white turtleneck, and her tan corduroy blazer. She'd be warm—and she didn't mind the fact that none of her skin would be showing either. She shivered with disgust at the thought that Mr. Conroy might actually have been checking her out before.

Elizabeth finished with her clothes and began fixing her hair. It would have been nice if Jessica had stayed around to lend her some moral support, but Elizabeth still hadn't told her sister what had happened. Besides, Jessica had a big date with Nick. Somehow she'd managed to wangle him into taking her to dinner at Andre's, and she'd been over at Lila Fowler's "getting dressed" since four o'clock.

Elizabeth was just finishing curling the tendrils

of hair she'd left free of her long French braid when there was a light knock on the door. "It's them," she said under her breath, switching off the curling iron. It seemed ridiculous to be so nervous about going somewhere with Tom, but that was how she felt. What if Mr. Conroy made another move on her? Worse, what if Tom saw him do it this time? Elizabeth wiped the damp palms of her hands on her blazer, took a deep breath, and opened the door. "Hi," she said brightly. "I'm all ready!"

"You look lovely," Mr. Conroy greeted her, smiling pleasantly.

"Really nice," Tom agreed.

"Uh, thanks. You both look nice too."

Tom was a little less dressed up than the night before, wearing khaki pants and a tweed jacket, but Mr. Conroy was wearing another formal suit. His light brown hair was combed straight back off his high forehead, giving him a sleek, clean appearance, and his dark eyes exactly matched his espresso-colored suit coat. He was a handsome man, Elizabeth realized suddenly, but of course she could never be interested in him.

"Should we go?" Mr. Conroy asked, nodding down the deserted dormitory hall.

"What? Oh! Of course." Elizabeth grabbed her purse and keys and stepped out into uncertainty, locking the door behind her.

The walk across campus was painfully slow

and awkward, but Elizabeth was the only one who seemed to notice. Tom chattered on and on, telling his father about the various stories they'd worked on at the news station. Elizabeth couldn't remember ever hearing him talk so much, but Mr. Conroy seemed truly interested and peppered Tom with questions. After what seemed like an eternity, they finally reached the amphitheater and took their seats. Elizabeth could barely wait for the music to begin so she could stop holding her breath.

The SVU open-air amphitheater was a popular place for concerts of all types. Famous rock bands played there frequently. But tonight the amphitheater had been taken over by student talent. The members of the student orchestra sat tuning their instruments onstage, looking ill at ease in their black concert suits and long dresses. The semicircular audience seating area was surprisingly crowded with students and parents, and the night was warmer than Elizabeth had expected. She had the feeling that when the lights went out, there would be a million stars overhead, and she started to relax a little.

"The Ninth is a pretty ambitious piece of music for students," Mr. Conroy commented as they flipped through their programs. "They must be good."

"They're *very* good," Tom said excitedly. "Elizabeth and I did a piece on them for WSVU that got picked up by the wire service. You should have seen . . ."

He was off again, but this time Elizabeth couldn't help smiling. What a motormouth! Mr. Conroy really brought out the best in Tom. Of course, now that she was seated right between them, it was a little harder for her to ignore the conversation.

"Tom," she said as soon as he paused for air. "Your dad must be tired of hearing about the station by now."

Mr. Conroy beamed at both of them from Elizabeth's other side. "Not at all," he said. "I'm fascinated."

That was all the encouragement Tom needed. He was just opening his mouth to launch into another tale of journalistic excellence when the lights went down and the crowd applauded politely.

"I'll tell you after," Tom promised Mr. Conroy quickly, settling back into his seat and taking Elizabeth's hand.

Elizabeth wasn't familiar with Beethoven's Ninth, and at first the music didn't reach her. It sounded unsettled, disjointed—just like her thoughts. If only she could get last night out of her mind! Of course, so far *this* evening Mr. Conroy hadn't done anything weird. . . .

"Have I told you today how beautiful you are?" Tom whispered in her ear, interrupting her thoughts.

"Yes, but tell me anyway," she answered. She snuggled into his shoulder, putting her cold hands beneath his right bicep.

"Maybe I should tell you how much I love you instead."

Elizabeth smiled. How could she have thought the music was disjointed? It was beautiful. "Maybe you should," she agreed happily.

And suddenly she felt foolish. All that stressing over nothing! It was a perfect evening, and Mr. Conroy was behaving like a perfect gentleman. Of *course* he wasn't interested in her—what kind of loser would hit on his own son's girlfriend? Elizabeth was only too glad that Tom didn't know what an idiot she'd been. She held his arm more tightly, giving herself over to the music.

An hour later the orchestra reached the "Ode to Joy" portion of the symphony and the SVU choir filed silently onto the stage, taking places behind the musicians. Elizabeth sat up straighter, surprised by the appearance of the singers. And then the singing began. Elizabeth couldn't remember ever hearing anything so amazing in her life.

The voices grew and swelled, claiming the night, peeling away two hundred years in their praise of a deaf composer. Elizabeth felt the gooseflesh raise on her arms and unexpected tears burned her eyes in acknowledgment of the music's perfect beauty. The voices came to a crescendo, and Elizabeth's heart rose up with them, soaring on the sound. It felt like . . . it felt like someone was rubbing up against her arm.

Mr. Conroy. Elizabeth's high spirits fell flaming back to earth as she felt him lean into her shoulder again. What did he think he was doing? She forced herself to look at him, but he only smiled back at her happily, as if nothing at all were wrong. He was swaying in time to the music, clearly enjoying himself.

He bumped into me by accident, Elizabeth told herself quickly. *He's just into the music.*

He bumped up against her again. *Accident. It was an accident!*

So why didn't she believe it?

Chapter Seven

Jessica sighed with satisfaction as the waiter put down her cut-crystal dessert plate. Before her was the type of dessert you'd see on a cooking show—the kind that looked as if someone had spent all day making it. A perfect round slice of chocolate mousse cake lay on a liquid tapestry of three different-colored dessert sauces, while a swath of carefully arranged fresh raspberries and chocolate leaves spilled across the cake slice and out to the edge of the plate.

"It's beautiful," she breathed, smiling at Nick. The truth was she didn't think she could eat another bite, but there was no way she was going to miss the entire Andre's experience.

Nick smiled back. "I'm glad you like it."

It had been an almost fairy-tale evening. Almost, because they'd come in Nick's Camaro instead of something more glamorous, like a limo.

But once they'd arrived at the restaurant, everything was perfect. Jessica looked around her at the sparkling dining room full of candles and champagne, trying to memorize every detail. She was suddenly *glad* that she'd never been to Andre's before—glad that she'd waited until a time in her life when she could truly appreciate it and elated that she'd come with Nick.

Impulsively Jessica reached across the intimate table for two and put her hand on Nick's. The diamond bracelet she'd borrowed from Lila glittered in the candlelight as Nick lifted her fingers to his mouth and kissed them. He was so handsome, he nearly took her breath away. She wondered what it would be like when they were both old—would she still feel the way she did tonight?

Whoa! she thought suddenly. *Back up the train!* Was she really thinking about growing old with this guy? She was! *I've fallen in love with him,* she realized in a slow panic. *What was I thinking?*

She must be insane—it was the only possible explanation. Withdrawing her hand from Nick's, Jessica pretended a sudden, consuming interest in eating her dessert. She *couldn't* be in love! Her relationships never worked out—everybody knew that. She was probably the worst, most unlucky judge of guys on the planet.

OK, what's wrong with him? she wondered,

looking up and studying Nick through narrowed blue-green eyes. If Jessica loved him, it followed that he must have some really major character flaw. But she couldn't think of a thing. Nick was sweet, he was exciting to be with, and he'd brought her to this outrageously expensive restaurant just to make her happy. All things considered, he was absolutely perfect. Jessica gave him a tentative smile, and Nick returned it with an intensity that made her feel suddenly weak. Oh, boy, was she ever in love.

You don't even know this guy! the part of her brain that was still thinking protested. But Jessica barely listened. That was a minor detail. She simply hadn't asked the right questions yet.

Jessica put down her silver dessert fork, unable to swallow another mouthful. "Nick," she said. "You know that guy at the movies yesterday? Where did you learn to fight like that?"

Nick started, as if surprised by the question, then shifted uncomfortably in his seat. "Oh, that." He laughed. "Chuck Norris movies, mostly."

"Be serious. It looked like you've had a lot of training."

"Uh, no. Not really."

Jessica knew he was lying. People who were telling the truth didn't squirm that way. "And what about those guys who chased us yesterday morning?" she asked. "Who were they?"

"Jessica, I already explained about that."

"A lot of guys grow up in bad neighborhoods without making people want to kill them," she pointed out reasonably. She pushed her cake plate away and leaned toward him over the table. Her blue-green eyes searched his dark green ones. "Who are you, really?" she asked.

"Uh, waiter!" Nick flagged the passing man over to their table as if it were a matter of national importance. "I'd like some coffee, please. How about you, Jessica?" he asked, turning back to the table. "Wouldn't you like some coffee?"

"An espresso," she said, never taking her eyes off his. He wasn't getting out of answering her questions that easily. She stared him down, biding the time it took for the waiter to return with their coffees. By the time the elaborate fuss of coffee and espresso, cream and sugar, spoons and saucers was complete, Nick was actually sweating.

"So, Nick," Jessica resumed smoothly. "I'm still waiting."

Nick gulped his coffee involuntarily, then set down his half-full cup so jerkily that the liquid sloshed into the saucer. "Would you like to dance?" he asked desperately.

Jessica smiled. He wasn't off the hook, but she could always pick this up again later. There was no way she was going to miss the chance to dance at Andre's. "Sure," she said, rising gracefully from the table.

Liz didn't dance, Jessica couldn't help thinking as Nick led her across the dining room to the polished oak dance floor. *I win.* She felt like a princess on the arm of her prince. The cranberry-colored, backless silk dress that Lila had loaned her was worth a fortune, and Nick looked incredible in his black bow tie and formal white jacket. There were only a few other couples on the dance floor, dancing to the gentle music from the live string ensemble, when Jessica stepped into Nick's arms and let him sweep her out across the gleaming wood.

He was an incredibly good dancer, smooth and confident. Jessica relaxed gradually into his arms, letting Nick and the music take her wherever she needed to go. It felt like flying, and she was sorry when the song ended.

"You dance as well as you fight," she remarked, smiling up into his face from her place in his arms. "Did you learn that from Chuck Norris movies too?"

"Fred and Ginger," Nick said uneasily, swinging back into motion as the music resumed.

Jessica held on tightly while they danced to song after song. It was the most romantic night of her life—no one had ever made her feel so special. She knew she should press Nick harder, should find out everything about him, but suddenly she didn't care anymore. She already knew she loved him. What else did she really need to know?

Still, she thought, opening her eyes just enough to watch the crystal chandeliers whirl by, *if I knew what he was up to, I could be a big help to him.* The thought excited her. She had a feeling she'd make the perfect spy. Besides, Nick had to be getting tired of evading her questions by now. Maybe if she just tried a little harder. One more question.

"Nick . . . ," she began, smiling sweetly.

Nick winced as Jessica lifted her head off his chest and smiled up at him.

"Why do you always carry a cellular phone?" she asked.

He'd known it was going to be something like that. She'd been bombarding him with questions half the evening. He'd hoped that taking her to a fancy restaurant would keep her satisfied for a while, but it seemed to be having the reverse effect. If anything, she was more curious than ever.

"So I can always call for a pizza," Nick joked. He drew her shining blond head back down to his chest and spun her possessively around the dance floor, struck by the way her loose golden ringlets spilled across his tuxedo shirt and contrasted with the dark red silk she wore. She was so beautiful. If only he *could* answer her questions! Nick felt as if his heart were tearing in two.

It just all seemed so unreal. A guy like him in a

place like Andre's with a girl like Jessica . . . Nick flinched involuntarily as he remembered exactly how unreal it was—he could never have afforded Andre's on his policeman's salary. Captain Wallace was going to have a four-way coronary when he saw the dinner bill and tuxedo rental on Nick's expense report.

"I want to request a song," Jessica said suddenly, lifting her head again. The ensemble was drawing to the end of the piece it was playing as Jessica strode across the dance floor to speak to the band leader. Nick watched as the elderly gentleman turned his head to see what she wanted, then did an obvious double take. Jessica was that stunning. Nick couldn't deny the jealousy he felt as he saw how the other man looked at her, even though the bandleader was probably old enough to be Jessica's grandfather.

"I asked them to play 'Fascination,'" Jessica reported, returning to his side. "Do you know that song?"

"I've heard it before." The strains from the violins floated across the dance floor, and Jessica floated into his arms as the band struck up the old torch song.

"I find *you* pretty fascinating," she told him.

"Watch out," he told her, paraphrasing the song, "fascination turns to love." His heart was suddenly in his throat as he waited to see how she'd respond.

"Too late," she teased.

Her words hit him like a jolt of electricity. Was it possible? Did she feel about him the way he felt about her? "Jessica," he said huskily, his voice thick with emotion. "There's something I have to tell you."

"Finally!" she exclaimed, gazing at him expectantly. She smiled by way of encouragement, and Nick knew that she thought he was going to tell her all his deep, dark secrets. *Not all,* he thought ruefully. *Only one.*

"I . . . I love you," he stammered, rushing ahead before she could interrupt. "I know we haven't known each other that long, and I know you're curious about my past. I wish I could tell you everything, but I can't. It's . . . it's for your own safety."

"I *knew* you were protecting me," she cried, pressing up against him. "Oh, Nick, tell me what's going on. I can help you!"

"No. It's too dangerous. As soon as I can tell you what's happening, I will. I promise you that. But for right now I'm just Nick Fox, SVU student."

Jessica didn't speak, and for a moment he thought she was mad at him. "I don't know," she said at last. "I guess I'm kind of fond of Nick Fox, SVU student. Is that your real name, at least?"

"Yes," he said with relief. "That's my real name."

"Mm-hm," Jessica said, raising her lips to his. "Then let's go back to the part where you tell me you love me."

Celine guided the little gray rental car through the narrow, dirty streets by the docks. This part of town always made her want to check her door locks, and she hated the thought that in a few minutes she'd have to abandon the car and set out on foot. She turned onto the last street before the harbor, parked at a vacant place next to the curb, and killed the engine—she'd walk the rest of the way. Even though she'd rented the car under an assumed name for extra security, Celine didn't want anyone taking down her license plate number.

It was quiet with the engine off, and Celine sat frozen in her seat a minute, her breathing shallow, distracted. *You have to calm down,* she told herself, consciously trying to relax. She couldn't see her knuckles through the black driving gloves she wore, but she knew that if she could, they'd be white. With an effort she pried her grip from the steering wheel and took several long, deep breaths. The night outside the car was very dark, very deserted, and this was by far the most dangerous part of her entire plan. Celine wished once again that she could have asked Jordan to do it for her, but she couldn't take a chance on Mr. Goody-Goody. Besides, she'd need him later.

Opening the driver's door in a rush, Celine stepped out into the blackness. The weather had been warm earlier, but the air was getting cold now. She huddled her shoulders together as a gust of wind cut through the unflattering, baggy blue sweatsuit she wore. The outfit was from the thrift store and would end up in a dumpster somewhere later in the evening, along with her secondhand sneakers. *And good riddance,* she thought, looking down at the uncharacteristically dowdy clothes with distaste. She pulled a floppy black hat down lower over her honey blond curls, making sure her hair was still tucked out of sight, before she locked the car door behind her.

"Here goes nothing," she breathed.

Walking quickly and purposefully, Celine cut across the dark street, then wound her way through the alleys and deserted parking lots toward the "visitors" part of the harbor. The main harbor was upscale and luxurious, but the visitors section, tucked away here at the farthest distance from the harbor mouth, was undeniably seedy. Celine quickened her steps still more, running along the seawall in search of Dock K.

An odor of salt, garbage, and rotting seaweed assailed her nostrils as she jogged toward the meeting place. It was a smell from a bad dream, and Celine could barely believe that she—a Louisiana Boudreaux—was actually somewhere so despicable. At night. By herself. "Peter better have come through," she muttered through gritted teeth as Dock K finally came into sight.

She'd learned about the man she was there to meet from her old friend Peter Wilbourne, and while Celine never questioned Peter's greed or malice, she frequently doubted his intelligence. Breathing hard, she stopped in the pool of light under a lamp at the entrance to the dock, waiting for the signal.

Luckily for her nerves, she didn't have to wait long. She'd been standing under the light just long enough to feel positively conspicuous when a man came down the seawall from the other direction. He fit the general description, and Celine hurried to light a cigarette, her hands shaking. She drew the hot smoke gratefully into her lungs, thankful for the calming effect it had on her. *Whoever invented this signal was a genius,* she thought, blowing a perfect smoke ring.

The man drew closer. He was wearing a navy blue pea coat and pants that could have been almost any light color once. A blue stocking cap covered his head, and as he stepped into the light Celine could see that his unshaven face was thin, deeply lined, and predatory. She felt a sharp stab of fear.

"Got a light?" the man asked.

"Sorry," she drawled, forcing her voice to stay calm. "I don't smoke." The signal was complete.

"Come on, then," her connection said gruffly, heading down the dock.

Celine hesitated for just a moment before flicking her cigarette off the seawall into the putrid water below, then followed him. *In for a penny, in for a pound,* her granny always said. Celine's heart hammered painfully as her new business partner reached the end of the dock and climbed aboard the most dilapidated boat there, motioning for her to come up beside him. No one knew where she was or what she was doing. The guy could be a mass murderer. . . . Celine forced every frightening thought from her mind and pulled herself up on deck.

The boat listed and rolled under their weight as the man in the pea coat moved to open the tiny cabin door. *It's a wonder this piece of junk even floats,* Celine thought, following her contact down the ladder from the hatch into the darkened living area below. Suddenly a light switched on and Celine gasped. There were three other men seated around a dining table in the dinky cabin, each one scarier than the last. The flashlights they were shining directly into her eyes kept Celine from making out their shadowy faces very well, but she saw enough to terrify her.

"You never said you were bringing anyone else," she accused the man she'd met first, her panic rising.

"You gotta problem widdat?" the largest guy at the table asked rudely. Not only were they criminals, they were illiterate criminals, an oddly detached portion of her brain noted clinically. What kind of people was she mixed up with?

"Not at all," Celine replied. She wondered if anyone else in the boat could hear her thundering heart. "Just give me my package and I'll be on my way."

The men around the table laughed, Celine's initial contact joining in from where he stood beside her, leaning against the ladder. "What do you think we are?" he asked. "Amateurs? Pull up a seat and we'll talk."

The last thing Celine wanted to do was sit down with those lowlifes, but the situation was rapidly slipping from her control. For just a second she considered fleeing back up the hatch and forgetting the whole thing, but Mr. Pea Coat was blocking the exit. *Besides,* she reminded herself, *how else will you get the money you need?* No, she'd come too far to back out now.

"Why, aren't you nice?" she cooed insincerely, perching on the edge of a filthy bunk. "What would y'all like to talk about?"

"How about money?" a second man at the table suggested, leaning forward into the beam from the flashlight he held. He was smaller and cleaner than the others, but there was something about his eyes that made Celine's breath catch in her chest. He looked like a stone-cold killer.

You are totally out of your league here, she told herself frantically, willing her body to breathe again. "How about it?" she replied lightly.

The killer leaned back a little, seemingly satisfied, but the big guy spoke up again. "You gotta smart mouth, you know dat?" he said loudly. For one horrifying moment it looked as if he was going to get up from the table, but the killer stopped him with an almost imperceptible movement of one hand. Celine felt a sensation like ice water trickling down her spine.

"We expect all the money to be delivered to us here within one week," said the third man at the table. "Minus your percentage, of course." Celine could see only enough to conclude that he was as bad as the others, but in spite of his rough, vulgar appearance his voice was smooth and cultivated—almost southern. Celine realized with a jolt that he must be the man she'd spoken to on the telephone when she'd set up this meeting.

"You'll have it," she said, trying to convey a confidence she didn't feel.

"Yeah. 'Cuz if we don't, see, den we'll have to kill you," Big Mouth informed her.

The killer smiled slightly, as if he relished the thought.

"You'll have it," Celine repeated, suppressing a shudder. She wanted out of there—fast. "Now, then, I'd love to stay here chatting with you gentlemen all night, but I have some other appointments."

A package the size of a large kitchen matchbox

sailed unexpectedly through the air and landed in her lap, causing her to jump with a mixture of surprise and fear. Celine looked down at the brown-paper-wrapped parcel without touching it, waiting for the men to stop laughing at her.

"Go ahead," the man in the pea coat invited at last. "Check it out. Test it if you want."

Celine picked up the package. "I'd rather not get into that here," she said, tucking it quickly into a fanny pack she was wearing cinched tight to her waist beneath the baggy sweatshirt. "I trust y'all."

The killer laughed—a humorless, grating sound.

"It's a wise woman who knows she has no choice," the smooth one agreed.

"Yes, well, I have to go now," Celine said, standing up. She half expected the pea coat to block her exit, but to her surprise, he moved out of her way. Celine climbed up the hatch hastily before he could change his mind.

"Ta-ta," the cultivated man called from below. "See you in a week."

She was dropping back over the gunwale when she heard it—Big Mouth's final comment. "Don't forget. We know where you live, *Celine.*"

They weren't supposed to know her name! She'd never told them her name. Celine's feet began racing down the rough wooden dock before she even realized she was running. What would they do to her if she didn't come through with the money? For that matter, what would happen to her if some lowlife lurking in the shadows caught her with the valuable package she was carrying? Fear finally overwhelmed Celine as she sprinted toward her rented car in an unseeing, headlong panic.

"That was amazing. Didn't you think so?" Elizabeth asked Tom and Mr. Conroy. Tom's talking streak seemed to have rubbed off on her as the three of them strolled back across campus after the concert. "I never knew I liked Beethoven so much."

Maybe if she kept on talking, no one would say anything she didn't want to hear. Not that Elizabeth really expected Mr. Conroy to say anything improper in front of Tom, but she wasn't in the mood to take chances either—especially not after all that awkward shoulder bumping. "What did you think, Tom?" she asked. "Wasn't it great?"

Tom barely looked at her as he directed his answer toward his father. "Yeah. I told you they're fantastic. You should have heard their spring series last year. That was when we did the news story on them."

"Maybe I can hear their series this year," Mr. Conroy said, beaming at Tom. "If they do another one."

"Oh yeah," Tom said excitedly. "They do it every spring."

Elizabeth was getting squeezed out of the conversation again. "Should we have some coffee?" she suggested. The night was clear and beautiful, but the weather had cooled considerably over the course of the concert. Elizabeth smiled apologetically. "I'm afraid my hands are freezing."

"Coffee sounds wonderful," Mr. Conroy agreed, much more enthusiastically than necessary. Didn't Tom notice it too? Elizabeth turned to look at him, but he was totally oblivious.

"Hey, George," Tom said. "We're going to be walking right by the station on our way to the coffeehouse. Why don't I run inside and get that story Elizabeth and I did on the orchestra? You can take it home and watch it on your VCR."

"Great!" Mr. Conroy slapped Tom on the back. "I'd really like to see all your work. Maybe you can pick out a few more tapes for me too."

Tom responded by throwing his chest out proudly and walking a little taller. The change in him over the last two days was incredible, and Elizabeth knew for certain that all of this newfound happiness was due to the appearance of his father. It killed her to think how hurt Tom would be if she was right about Mr. Conroy.

The rest of the way to the television station Tom kept up a running chatter. He talked mostly about his past work at WSVU but managed to digress into his old football career, his plans for the following summer, and a story about a pet frog he'd had when he was eight years old along the way.

Elizabeth had never heard him talk so openly. When she'd been trying to get to know Tom, it was like pulling teeth to get him to reveal even the most trivial things, but now he was spilling his guts to a man he barely knew. *It's great that he's already so close to his father,* Elizabeth told herself, trying to focus on the positive. It *was* great, but it was also scary.

"I'll just run in and get those tapes," Tom said as the group reached the concrete patio area at the front of the station building. "I'll be right back."

"Wait!" Elizabeth said frantically. She didn't want to be left alone with Mr. Conroy.

Tom and his father both turned to look at her, clearly surprised by the panic in her voice.

"I mean, let's all go," she suggested weakly. "I'm sure your father would like to see the station."

"No, wait here—I'll only be a minute." Tom pushed his way through the heavy entry doors and took off running toward the WSVU offices.

"I saw the station yesterday," Mr. Conroy explained.

"Oh. And what did you think of it?" Standing alone with Mr. Conroy in the cold night air make Elizabeth feel even more nervous and awkward than before. *Hurry up, Tom,* she prayed silently.

"I liked it a lot. You must all be very talented."

Elizabeth laughed tensely. "Well, your son is anyway."

"I'm sure he is," Mr. Conroy said. "And I'm sure you're just as talented." He took a step closer.

"Oh no. Not really." *Hurry up, Tom!*

"I love it that you're so modest." He took another step forward. "It's very attractive."

"Mr. Conroy . . ."

"Here, I want to give you something."

Before Elizabeth could finish the protest she'd begun, Mr. Conroy took a small box from inside his coat pocket and pressed it into her hands. "It's a gift," he explained. "To thank you for bringing me and Tom together."

"You shouldn't have," she replied, surprised.

Elizabeth looked down at the small gift-wrapped box in her hands with an overwhelming sense of relief. All Mr. Conroy wanted was to give her a present! Thank goodness she hadn't said anything stupid. She held the box up into the light, admiring the deep blue paper imprinted with crescent moons and stars and the pinkish white iridescent ribbon. "It's so pretty. Did you wrap it yourself?"

Instead of answering, Mr. Conroy reached out and grabbed her by both wrists. "If I could, I'd give you the *real* moon and stars," he said fervently, a lovesick look in his eyes.

"What?" She tried to pull her hands away, but he held on.

"Listen to me, Elizabeth. I know you're dating my son—"

"That's right!" she interrupted, struggling to break free.

"But I can't live without you. I know it's wrong, but I'm a weak person, Elizabeth. You make me feel strong." He released her hands, only to grab her shoulders instead.

"Stop it! Mr. Conroy!"

He leaned forward, bringing his face toward hers. He was going to kiss her! Elizabeth pushed with all her strength, breaking Mr. Conroy's embrace and forcing him backward several steps across the pavement.

"Elizabeth . . . ," he began plaintively, moving toward her again.

"Stay away from me," she warned, her voice shaking with outraged emotion.

Just then the front door of the television station burst open. "So!" Tom said, juggling far more tapes than he could carry safely. "This ought to get you started, George. And there are plenty more where these came from."

"Super," Mr. Conroy said smoothly, moving to

relieve Tom of half the tapes. "I'm looking forward to seeing them."

Elizabeth stood to one side in shocked disbelief. Was Mr. Conroy really going to act as if nothing had happened? And Tom—had he really seen nothing? Elizabeth's heart was pounding and her hands shook violently. Looking down, she saw that her right hand still clutched Mr. Conroy's unopened gift. Quickly, without thinking, she stuffed it into her blazer pocket. She'd figure out what to do about the gift later, but she clearly couldn't return it in front of Tom.

"Are we ready, then?" Mr. Conroy asked jovially. "How about that coffee, Elizabeth?"

"You . . . you'll have to excuse me," Elizabeth stammered. "I . . . I have a stomachache all of a sudden."

"Are you OK, Liz?" Tom asked, looking concerned.

"Fine. I . . . I'll see you tomorrow."

Elizabeth could hear the two men talking about her as she hurried away across the quad, but she couldn't stay a second longer. How dare Mr. Conroy grab her like that? And then to pretend that nothing was wrong in front of Tom! It made her skin crawl. Unshed tears burned her eyelids as Elizabeth hurried through the chilly night toward Dickenson Hall and the sanctuary of her room.

Elizabeth let herself into the darkened dorm room with relief and turned on a desk light. She had dared to hope that her sister might be home to talk to, but the room was empty. Jessica's side looked like a half-off bin on the last day of a lingerie sale—as usual—and her bed was unmade. Apparently she was still out on her big date at Andre's, and knowing Jessica, Elizabeth thought, she'd probably milk it for all it was worth.

"I doubt I'll see her before tomorrow," Elizabeth muttered, taking off her jacket and hanging it over the back of her desk chair. It was then that she noticed Mr. Conroy's gift still peeking from the pocket. "What am I going to do about this?" She groaned aloud, lifting the tiny box from her blazer and sitting on the edge of her bed with it. In the light of her room the moons and stars on the paper sparkled metallically and the ribbon looked like the Milky Way. "I don't know whether it would be worse to keep it or give it back!"

She sat for a while, pondering the alternatives. Whatever it was, she didn't want it. But at least if she kept it, she'd be spared having to see Mr. Conroy again when she returned it. But would she be able to avoid him forever? "I might as well see what it is," she said at last, stripping off the paper in one quick, decided motion.

Under the wrapping was a small gray velvet jewelry box. *Oh no,* she thought, popping the expensive-looking lid apprehensively. A tiny slip of white paper fell from the box and fluttered to her bedspread, but Elizabeth didn't look at it immediately—her eyes were glued to the contents of the box. Inside the elegant gray velvet reposed a golden, heart-shaped locket with a solid pavé of real diamonds. It was breathtaking, and Elizabeth knew it must have cost plenty. Dazed, she reached down for the slip of white paper, tearing her eyes from the locket to read:

You should have diamonds. Love, George

Elizabeth dropped the note and the locket as if she'd been bitten. "How dare he!" she exclaimed. To eavesdrop on her and Tom and then to *steal* something romantic Tom had said for his own twisted purposes—it was perverse. Quickly, blindly, Elizabeth gathered up the note and the locket and stuffed them into her desk, slamming the drawer with a bang. She never wanted to see them *or* George Conroy again.

Chapter Eight

The persistent loud ring of the telephone gradually wormed its way into Jessica's dreams. *Who would be rude enough to call this early?* she wondered, annoyed, as the phone continued to shrill. Jessica pulled a pillow over her head. She'd been up at the crack of dawn the last two mornings in a row—she *deserved* to sleep in.

"*Get* it, Liz," she whined from under the pillow, but the phone kept ringing. Elizabeth must have already left for class, Jessica realized.

"All *right!*" she cried at last, throwing her pillow across the room. "This had better be good." She sprang out of bed and snatched the receiver from the hook. "Hello?"

"Jessica?" Tom Watts said. "Hi. Is Elizabeth there?"

"Of course not . . . ," Jessica began, turning her head toward Elizabeth's bed and expecting to see it already perfectly made up. But to Jessica's surprise, Elizabeth was still in it, motioning frantically that she wasn't. "Uh, just a minute, Tom," Jessica said, putting her hand over the phone. "What's up?" she whispered to her twin.

"Say I'm not here," Elizabeth whispered back urgently. "No, wait! Say I'm still asleep. Say I'm sick!"

Jessica shrugged. "Whatever." She took her hand off the mouthpiece. "Tom? Liz is still in bed—I don't think she feels very well." She listened for a minute. "OK," she said, then hung up the phone.

"What did he want?" Elizabeth asked immediately.

"To talk to you, obviously," Jessica answered, looking at her sister. Elizabeth was sitting up in bed now, wearing only an ugly flannel nightgown and a very worried expression. "What's going on, anyway?" Jessica asked, jumping back into her own bed and huddling under the covers. Her black satin shorty pajamas were much more stylish than Elizabeth's outfit, but they weren't very warm.

"Oh, Jess." Elizabeth groaned, putting a hand to her forehead. "I don't even know where to start."

"Did you and Tom have a fight?"

"No. Not at all. It's his father."

"You had a fight with Mr. Conroy?" Jessica asked, surprised. She'd thought Mr. Conroy was perfect in her sister's book.

"Not exactly a fight. He wants to date me."

Jessica sat staring at the tragic expression on her twin's face for about fifteen seconds before she broke out laughing. "You're insane," she gasped between peals. "Mr. Conroy?"

"I'm not kidding!" Elizabeth protested, becoming indignant. "He was acting really strange the night before last at Andre's, then last night he tried to kiss me!"

"Stop it, Liz! You're killing me," Jessica cried, holding her sides. No doubt her sister was totally overreacting, as usual. "You must have misunderstood."

"Oh yeah?" Elizabeth said, her blue-green eyes flashing. Rising, she grabbed something out of her desk drawer and threw it at Jessica. "Misunderstand this!"

"Ow!" Jessica complained as a gray jewelry box hit her in the elbow. "What's that?"

"Open it," Elizabeth ordered grimly.

Jessica snapped open the lid and gasped in amazement. "Oh, wow. It's totally gorgeous." Her mind raced as she imagined all the important future occasions she'd be borrowing the necklace for.

"Read the note," Elizabeth instructed, calling her back to the present.

Jessica read: "*You should have diamonds. Love, George*. Who's George?" she asked.

"Mr. Conroy!" Elizabeth practically shouted.

"Oh," Jessica said, her visions of borrowed diamonds shattered. "Yuck. What kind of freak gives his son's girlfriend jewelry?"

"The *same* kind of freak who wants to go out

with her," Elizabeth answered, clearly exasperated.

"Well, who knew?" Jessica defended herself. "You have to admit, it sounds pretty far-fetched."

"I know," Elizabeth admitted, burying her face in her hands. "It's a total nightmare."

"So does Tom know?"

"No, and I can't tell him—he'd be crushed."

Jessica thought for a minute. "I think you have to tell him anyway, Elizabeth. I mean, you can't let things go on like this."

Elizabeth looked up. "I know, but I made my feelings pretty clear to Mr. Conroy last night. Maybe he'll give up."

Jessica shrugged. "Maybe." She didn't actually believe that a man who'd crossed so far over the line—not to mention spent that kind of money—was going to give up easily. Still, it might be time to change the subject.

"You haven't asked me about my date with Nick last night," Jessica reminded her sister.

Elizabeth climbed out of bed and started rummaging through her closet. "How was it?" she asked, not sounding very interested.

"Perfect," Jessica enthused, remembering Nick's arms around her on the dance floor with a hot flush of pleasure. "Nick was a perfect gentleman. We had an incredible time."

"That's nice," Elizabeth said vaguely. She left the closet and began digging through her dresser drawers.

Jessica knew her sister wasn't really listening, but she didn't care. She couldn't remember the last time she'd felt so good about being with a guy. "I really think Nick's the one, Elizabeth," she said.

That got her attention. "What?" Elizabeth demanded, midrummage. "He's the *what?*"

Jessica fell backward into her pillows, hugging herself. "We're in love," she announced.

"Oh, brother." Elizabeth walked over to sit on the edge of her sister's bed. "Are you sure?"

"Of course I'm sure!" Jessica wasn't going to let her sister's sour mood spoil her own. "He's totally romantic and gorgeous and sweet and . . ." She paused, searching for just the right adjective.

"And weird," Elizabeth supplied.

"He is not!" Jessica bristled. "How can you say that?"

"Jess, the guy walks all over campus with his ear glued to a cell phone. Nina and I saw him yesterday making calls in the middle of the football fields. Don't you think that's a little strange?"

"Not at all," Jessica said breezily. If that was the best Elizabeth could do, then Jessica had nothing to worry about.

"Well, what's up with that?" Elizabeth demanded.

How could Jessica tell her when she wasn't exactly sure herself? All she knew for certain was that the phone was important—it was the key, in fact. If it weren't for the cell phone, how would Jessica have found out that Nick had a pickup scheduled for seven o'clock that very night? And if she hadn't found out, how would she be there to learn all his secrets? The night before, at Andre's, Nick had promised to tell her everything about himself as soon as he could—but why wait? By seven-thirty tonight all Jessica's questions would be answered.

Jessica smiled at her sister with total confidence. "I'll tell you tomorrow," she promised.

"Alex!" Doug exclaimed. "Boy, am I glad to see you!"

Alex laughed and shrugged her heavy book bag off into one of the chairs in the hot-line lobby. "Thanks, I'm glad to see you too." She had an hour-long break between classes, so she'd decided to drop by again to see if she could help.

"No, really," Doug said, looking frantic. "Remember that test I mentioned yesterday? Well, it's today, and I don't have a clue what I'm doing. Could you possibly cover the phones for me so I can go cram in the library?"

"Sure," Alex agreed, surprised but pleased that Doug already trusted her enough to leave her on her own for an entire hour. "I'd be glad to."

"You're a lifesaver," he said, gathering up his books. "I owe you."

"No problem," Alex assured him as he barreled out the door. She smiled to herself when Doug was gone. "I'm a lifesaver," she repeated happily, putting on her headset.

She hadn't been waiting long when her first call came in.

"SVU Substance Abuse Hot Line," Alex said, flipping the switch.

"Uh, hi," said a male voice at the other end. "I was wondering if I could ask you a question." The guy sounded completely frazzled.

"Of course," Alex said warmly. "Ask me anything."

"I don't know if this is strictly your area, but you guys are the *substance* abuse hot line and all. I . . . uh, I was wondering—are there a lot of drugs on this campus?"

The question took Alex by surprise. "Well, I don't know if there are a *lot*," she answered, "but there are some. Why do you ask?"

"Oh, no reason," her caller said.

Yeah, right, Alex thought, waiting to see if he'd illuminate her.

"It's just that, well . . . are these calls confidential?"

"Of course."

"Well, I . . . I think I might be involved in a drug deal here on campus. I'm not *sure*," he rushed to add, "but I might be."

Alex didn't know what to say. The call didn't fit any of the patterns she and Doug had gone over.

"I don't understand," she admitted at last. "How can you be involved in a drug deal and not know it?"

"Well, there's this girl," the caller said.

"Actually I guess she's kind of my girlfriend." Now that he'd finally gotten started, he seemed eager to explain. "Anyway, she wants me to meet this guy on campus and sell him some kind of package. She says it's just papers, but I don't really believe that."

"You don't trust her?" Alex asked.

"I don't *know* her. I only met her a couple of days ago."

Alex's head was spinning. The whole thing seemed nuts, but she had to stay impartial if she was going to be any help.

"If you're not comfortable with what she's asking you to do, then you shouldn't do it," Alex advised, figuring she couldn't go wrong with that.

"But what if she gets mad and doesn't want to see me anymore?" the caller asked. He was starting to sound desperate again.

"Do you think she'd do that?"

"I don't know," he said miserably. "I only know I can't give her up."

"But if you've only just met her—" Alex began.

"You don't understand!" he interrupted. "Guys like me don't *meet* girls like her. I'll never have another girlfriend this amazing in my life."

"I . . . I don't know what to say," Alex said at last. "I wish you wouldn't do this deal—whatever it is—but I can't tell you what to do."

"Yeah, I know." He sounded totally defeated.

"Will you at least promise me one thing?" Alex

asked, genuinely worried for him. "Will you call me again after it's over and tell me what happened?"

"I don't know. . . ." The caller hesitated.

"I'd just like to know you're OK," Alex said quickly. "That's the only reason I'm asking."

"Well, all right," he agreed. "But I better go now."

Alex disconnected the line and sat staring into space, unable to shake the spooky feeling the call had given her. Whatever was going to happen, it seemed pretty clear that her caller was only peripherally involved. But what if it really *was* a drug deal and he got caught? Would he go to jail to protect this new girlfriend of his? And what was Alex supposed to do? If she had possible knowledge of a crime and didn't report it to the police, did that make her an accessory?

"Oh, Doug." She groaned, wishing he hadn't left her alone after all. "Where are you when I really need you?"

Thinking of Doug gave Alex an idea—she'd try to imagine what Doug would do if he were in her shoes. She'd no sooner had the thought than she had the answer: *I hope this goes without saying, but anything you hear here is one hundred percent confidential. It doesn't leave this room, no matter what.* That was what Doug had told her before he'd let her monitor her very first call.

Alex knew then that she wasn't going to tell *anyone* about the call she'd just taken. She couldn't.

* * *

"I hope you have some good news for me," Captain Wallace bellowed as soon as he picked up the receiver.

Nick moved the cell phone an inch away from his ear. He was standing under some bleachers at the edge of the athletics fields, but the reception between him and the police station was still, unfortunately, excellent.

"I wish I did," Nick told his superior officer. "I've got a meet tonight, but I don't expect much."

"What meeting?" the chief barked irritably. Nick could hear him shuffling reams of paperwork impatiently in the background. "I don't have any notes here about a meeting."

"No," Nick agreed. "I didn't call it in. The guy sounds like a total nutcase—I doubt he'll come through."

"I don't care!" Captain Wallace exploded. "If there's a meeting, this office has to know about it. I don't want a repeat of Sunday, and I *don't* want you running around out there like the Lone Ranger. You got me, Fox?"

"Yes, sir," Nick responded quickly. The chief was right, of course—even losers could be dangerous. "I'm sorry, sir."

"Damn right you're sorry," the chief grumbled, somewhat placated. "You can kiss my butt for the rest of the week anyway."

"Always a pleasure, sir," Nick joked weakly.

He'd have to wait a couple of *months* to turn in his expense report now.

"So what's the setup?" Captain Wallace asked. "Let's have the details."

"Seven o'clock, behind the science building. That's all I know. It was some new guy who made the call—I don't know who he is and I don't know who's coming for the actual buy."

"You don't know much, do you, Fox?" the chief asked, but Nick could tell he wasn't quite as mad anymore. It was all part of the captain's tough-guy act.

"I'm afraid not, sir. Like I said, I wouldn't get my hopes up for this one. The guy was rambling on about secret documents and animal testing and all kinds of whacked-out stuff."

"Well, it's better than nothing. Is everything in place at your end?"

"Yes, sir. Everything's a go."

"All right, then, Fox. I'll take care of things here. You call back in after the meet."

The chief hung up without waiting for Nick's answer. They both knew it was academic anyway. If the chief said call, then Nick would call. Police work wasn't the kind of job you did when you felt like it. There were laws, and on top of the laws there were rules and chains of command. No matter how much he might not like it sometimes, Nick had to do whatever Captain Wallace and the law said. He had no choice.

*   *   *

"Celine! Are you in there? Open the door!"

The loud, unexpected pounding on her apartment door gave Celine such a jolt of adrenaline that she thought she might vomit. What were *they* doing here? It was only Tuesday! Celine cowered on her small sofa, expecting the door to be kicked in any minute.

"Celine, it's Jordan. Open up! I'm not kidding."

Jordan! That idiot almost scared her to death. She'd been sure it was the men from the boat.

"I'm coming," she said irritably, rising. "Don't get your shorts in a bunch." Celine glanced involuntarily toward the kitchen as she moved to answer the door. The package was hidden in her toaster oven, wrapped up in foil like a hunk of old bread.

"What's all this ruckus about?" she asked, opening the door. She glanced quickly up and down the hall to make sure no one was looking, then pulled Jordan inside and locked the door behind him.

"We've got to talk, Celine," he said. Jordan's forehead was drawn into deep creases between his eyebrows, and he was even paler than usual. His chest heaved erratically as he struggled to control his breathing, while his barely blue eyes looked almost frantic.

"If you say so, sugar," she purred, pouring on the charm. It didn't take a genius to see the guy was having major second thoughts. "We can talk. *Or* we can do anything you want." She pressed up against him suggestively, but he brushed her aside and went to sit on the sofa, burying his troubled face in his hands.

Celine was miffed in spite of her total lack of interest in the guy. Who did he think he was? Still, she needed him for a few more hours—as hard as it was, she'd have to swallow her pride and be nice to him. After Jordan did the deal with Nick tonight, she'd cut him loose in a millisecond. She'd enjoy it, in fact.

"What do you want to talk about, darling?" Celine dropped onto the sofa next to Jordan, putting a hand on his skinny thigh and drawing herself in very close. He was wearing jeans with rips in the knees and a rumpled red shirt, and he looked as if he hadn't slept in two days. "Is it about us?"

Jordan ran his hands distractedly through his cropped blond hair, making it stand on end, and Celine realized it was the first time she'd ever seen him venture out in public without his baseball hat.

"Celine," he said at last. "I really like you—and I want us to be together. But you've got to tell me what's in that package I'm selling tonight."

"Why, Jordan!" Celine exclaimed, hoping she sounded delighted. "Isn't that so sweet? I like you too, sugar."

Unfortunately Jordan was too worked up to be so easily distracted. "Then tell me what's in the package," he begged, taking her hands in his and meeting her eyes straight on for the first time ever. "I have to know, Celine."

For a second she almost felt sorry for him. He was so innocent and sincere, so completely without a clue. But then the feeling passed.

"I already told you," she lied. "It's papers from my brother's work. Remember?"

"I remember you said that, Celine, but are you sure it isn't drugs?"

"Drugs!" She pulled her hands from his in one rough motion, staring as if she'd been slapped in the face.

"I know you'd never get mixed up in anything like that on purpose," Jordan assured her, "but how about these other people? Isn't it possible that—"

"I think I know my own brother, Jordan Wilson," Celine told him indignantly, cutting him off in midsentence. "How dare you suggest—"

"No, Celine!" Jordan interrupted her in turn. "I'm not suggesting anything."

She pouted, her face turned down toward the sofa cushions. "It sure sounded like it," she said in a wounded tone.

"I'm just concerned, that's all." Jordan ducked his head to try to look into her face. "For *both* of us."

Celine made her eyes big and stricken. "But baby," she asked, "don't you want to help poor animals in danger?"

"Of course!" he said. "Sure I do." He looked tired and confused.

She let him take her hands again. "Then why are we fighting?" she asked tremulously.

"We're not fighting! Oh, Celine, don't cry. Of course I'll do it. I was going to do it anyway. Please don't cry, Celine."

Celine put her arms around Jordan's shoulders, burying her face against his neck. She always found she got more mileage out of crocodile tears when they made the other person wet.

"Come on, Celine," Jordan begged, patting her back awkwardly. "Don't cry."

She sniffled theatrically. "What do you expect?" she asked. "We were getting along so well and now everything's ruined."

"Ruined? No! What are you talking about?"

"You're not mad at me?"

"Mad at *you*? Of course not!" Jordan lifted her tear-streaked face from his neck and looked deeply into her eyes. "I . . . I think I love you, Celine."

"Oh, baby!" she breathed, bringing her lips to his in a passionate kiss.

That little confession was going to come in very handy.

Chapter Nine

Elizabeth stood outside the door to Nina's physics classroom, nervously chewing her bottom lip. It was almost two o'clock, and she'd missed all her own classes. Elizabeth hadn't meant to ditch, but every time she'd started to get ready to go, she'd discovered that she wasn't able to leave her room. Instead she'd stayed in the dorm all day, worrying about Mr. Conroy's advances.

"Hi, Elizabeth." A girl Elizabeth knew vaguely from a PE class passed her in the hall and Elizabeth waved. *Good,* she thought, *classes are starting to let out.*

The door to the physics room burst open, providing a means of exit for a stampede of students. Elizabeth strained up on her toes, looking for Nina in the overfull auditorium. "Nina!" she called, waving, when she spotted her friend. Nina stood out from the crowd in a bright yellow top and matching pair of shorts, which looked great against her dark skin. Elizabeth glanced down at her own I'm-in-a-bad-mood outfit of a baby T-shirt, windbreaker, and SVU sweatpants and wished briefly that she'd made a bigger fashion effort before she pushed the subject of clothing from her mind.

"Nina, hi!" Elizabeth called again, waving over her friend.

"Hi," Nina answered, making her way through the crowd to Elizabeth's side at last. "How are you?"

Elizabeth rolled her eyes and groaned. "Don't ask."

"Mr. Conroy?" Nina guessed. She leaned against the wall in the hallway and balanced her already full backpack on one knee while she tried to stuff her ten-pound physics textbook into it.

"And how!" Elizabeth said, reaching to help Nina with the book. "Listen, I hate to dump on you two days in a row, but do you have time to talk?" Elizabeth nodded down the hall in the general direction of the cafeteria. "I'll buy you a coffee," she coaxed.

Nina laughed. "I always have time to get dumped on by a friend," she teased. "*Especially* if you want to throw in one of those big, gooey brownies with that coffee."

Elizabeth smiled gratefully, and she and Nina began walking in the direction of the cafeteria.

There was no one Elizabeth would rather have talked to about her problem. Nina was always a careful, caring listener who gave solid advice. Besides, Jessica certainly hadn't been any help. After bending Elizabeth's ear mercilessly with more tales of Nick the Wonder Boyfriend, she'd complained about Celine for an hour, then run off to have a late breakfast with Lila. Elizabeth hadn't seen her since.

"So, what's going on with Mr. Conroy?" Nina asked as they took seats in a corner of the mostly empty cafeteria. "Did he do something else?" She popped the lid on her Styrofoam cup of coffee and stirred in some creamer before taking a bite of an enormous brownie with deep swirls of chocolate frosting.

"He tried to kiss me," Elizabeth said miserably, her eyes glued to Nina's brownie. It would be so easy to throw herself a pity fest and eat two or three of those. With an immense effort Elizabeth forced her gaze back to the black coffee in front of her.

"He did not!" Nina exclaimed. "When?"

"Last night. After the concert." Elizabeth groaned again. "Oh, Nina, it was so awful."

"Wow," Nina said, taking another bite. "What are you going to do?"

Elizabeth didn't answer right away, and Nina eventually looked up from her plate. "Is this brownie bothering you?" she asked, finally seeming to notice the way Elizabeth was watching her eat. Elizabeth had struggled with her weight ever since she'd come to college, but she'd had it under control for a long time now. In fact, she and Nina usually dieted together. "You *know* this is going to be my dinner," Nina added, smiling, "but I'll split it with you if you want."

"No, thanks," Elizabeth said, trying her best to return her friend's warm smile. "I shouldn't."

"So, what are you going to do about Mr. Conroy?" Nina repeated.

"I don't know," Elizabeth admitted, shaking her head. "I guess I should tell Tom, but how can I when he's so happy? It'll break his heart."

"Yeah," Nina agreed. "That doesn't sound like such a hot idea."

"But what else can I do? I mean, I can try to avoid him, but sooner or later Tom's going to catch on. Plus I'm afraid that the longer I let things go, the harder it will be."

"For who?" Nina asked astutely.

"For me," Elizabeth admitted. "But for Tom too. He's getting more attached to that man every day."

"Well, he *is* Tom's father," Nina pointed out.

"Don't remind me." Elizabeth dropped her face into her hands. The way things were going, she could almost wish she'd never gotten involved in helping Mr. Conroy look for his son in the first place.

"Maybe you could talk to Mr. Conroy," Nina suggested, polishing off the brownie and turning her attention to her coffee.

"Yeah, right." Elizabeth reached into the pocket of her turquoise windbreaker and pulled out the velvet jewelry box. Without a word she opened the lid and set the glittering diamond locket down in front of Nina.

"Oh, my." Nina's eyes widened as she lifted the necklace to the light. "Are those real?"

"Yep. A little present from Mr. Conroy."

"Liz! You can't keep that!"

"Of course I can't," Elizabeth agreed. "But how am I going to return it without seeing Mr. Conroy again? Give it to Tom?"

"You should give it back to Mr. Conroy yourself," Nina said decidedly, "and tell him you're not interested. I don't see why you even need to involve Tom."

"What?" Elizabeth gasped with surprise. "Not involve Tom? Wouldn't that be dishonest?"

"You don't want to hurt Tom, right?" Nina argued. "And why should you when there's no reason you can't handle this yourself? Make Mr. Conroy understand that you don't appreciate his attention and tell him to stop it."

"Do you really think that will work?" Elizabeth asked. Her mind ran over Nina's suggestion, looking for flaws. It would be great if the situation could be resolved so easily, but it didn't seem likely.

"I don't see why not," Nina insisted. "You're both adults. And it's reasonable to assume that Mr. Conroy doesn't want to throw away his relationship with Tom."

"Yes," Elizabeth agreed thoughtfully.

"In fact, I'll bet in a few weeks this entire thing will be completely forgotten," Nina predicted, jabbing her coffee stirrer in the air for emphasis.

Elizabeth raised an eyebrow. "Let's not get carried away, Nina. *I'm* not going to forget it."

"Well, OK. Maybe not forgotten, but *forgiven.* I mean, if he's willing to apologize and leave you alone, aren't you willing to drop it?"

"Yeah," Elizabeth said, imagining what an enormous relief that would be. "Gladly."

Nina smiled. "Then get going, girl."

"And you should see Nick *dance,*" Jessica told anyone who'd listen in the Theta parlor. She'd been describing her dream date at Andre's for the last half hour. "He's by far the best dancer I've ever gone out with."

A couple of the girls rolled their eyes, but Jessica didn't care—they were just jealous. She smiled at them regally from her place in the middle of the largest sofa.

"Well, at least he didn't step on my dress," Lila said from Jessica's right side. "That's a Giovanni original from Italy." The former Countess di Mondicci dipped a carrot stick into some yogurt dressing, then sat staring into space without eating it. "Are you still going to pick up that hat for me tonight?" she asked.

"Lila!" Jessica complained. "Enough with the hat, already! I said I would."

Denise Waters smiled at Lila from her wing chair across the coffee table from the sofa. "What's the hat for?"

"I have to go to brunch at Bruce's parents' house tomorrow," Lila explained. "I just want to look good."

"You *always* look good, Lila," Denise said sincerely.

Lila smiled weakly. "Thanks."

"Hello!" Jessica interrupted. "Can we forget about the stupid hat for five minutes? I'm trying to tell you about Nick."

"You mean there's *more?*" Denise asked.

In Jessica's opinion, she didn't look nearly as thrilled as she should have. "Yes, there's more," Jessica shot back. "I think he's a government agent!"

Denise looked at Jessica in surprise, then burst out laughing. "Whose government?" she asked.

"Ours, of course," Jessica answered, annoyed.

"Now I've heard everything," Alison Quinn called from across the room.

Jessica shot her an evil look, then turned back to her friends. "I mean it," she said in a much lower voice. "It all adds up."

"If you say so." Denise was still laughing and Lila had joined her.

"You go ahead and laugh," Jessica said irately. "But tomorrow you'll both be begging my pardon."

"I doubt it," Lila gasped between giggles.

"It so happens that Nick has a crucial meeting tonight," Jessica said importantly. "But unfortunately he's going to be unexpectedly detained, and *I'll* be there instead."

"What are you talking about?" Denise wanted to know.

"I overheard him on his cellular phone," Jessica whispered excitedly to the two other girls. "He's supposed to meet someone tonight, and he doesn't know I know about it. I'm going to sabotage his car and go in his place."

"What?" Lila squeaked. She wasn't laughing now. "Are you *crazy*? What if it's those guys who chased you in the Jeep on Sunday?"

"Why?" Denise protested almost simultaneously. "What's the point?"

"The point," Jessica answered triumphantly, "is to find out all about him. He's not allowed to tell me about his job, but that doesn't mean I can't do a little poking around on my own."

"Oh, a relationship built on trust," Denise said scornfully.

"No, a relationship built on excitement," Jessica countered. "Something you wouldn't know about with *Winston!*"

Denise's blue eyes flashed. "I'll have you know that being with Winston is *very* exciting."

"Sure, it is," Jessica agreed. "If he's drinking grape juice and you're wearing white." Jessica's old high-school friend Winston Egbert was by far the biggest klutz she knew.

"You'll never have a man as good as Winston," Denise fired back angrily. Her voice had risen to the point that several of their Theta sisters turned to look.

"Come on, you two," Lila broke in. "You're making a scene. Anyway, look, here comes Isabella."

"Isabella!" Jessica called happily as her friend entered the room. "Come sit with us!" *Isabella* would want to hear about Nick.

"Hi, everyone," Isabella Ricci greeted them, taking a seat on the couch on Jessica's other side. "What's up?"

Jessica had her mouth half open, ready to tell Isabella all about Nick, but Lila spoke first. "Nothing that interesting," she said, shooting a cease-and-desist glance at Jessica. "What's up with you?"

"Ugh," Isabella said, stretching her tan legs out in front of her and kicking off her high-heeled sandals. "I just saw Celine in the bookstore and she said she was on her way over here next. Enjoy the peace and quiet while you can."

The other girls in the little group groaned. "I

wish we hadn't let her into the sorority," Lila said. "What a mess."

"You're not kidding," Isabella agreed. "Well, look on the bright side—maybe she won't come through with the decorating she promised to do and we can kick her out again."

"I wish," Jessica said. If it weren't for Nick, she'd have been totally depressed about Celine.

"I'd pay for the decorating myself if I thought it would keep her out," Lila said. "Like my daddy always says, fight money with money."

"I thought the expression was 'fight fire with fire,'" Denise corrected.

"Same thing," Lila agreed, smiling smugly.

"Oh, yuck. Here she comes," Isabella broke in, barely nodding toward the door.

"Celine!" Alison Quinn's false soprano cut through the room with all the euphony of fingernails on a chalkboard. "I'm so glad you made it! Here, come and sit with us." The Theta vice president rose to give Celine her own favorite seat, taking a smaller chair by the fireplace instead.

All four girls in Jessica's group could barely disguise their disgust.

"I hate that evil little witch," Jessica whispered through gritted teeth.

"Which one?" Lila asked, looking from Celine to Alison.

"Take your pick."

* * *

Elizabeth stood uncertainly on the plush, champagne-colored carpeting, working up her nerve to use Mr. Conroy's polished brass knocker. Nina had made talking to Tom's father seem like such an easy, obvious solution that Elizabeth had hurried from the cafeteria, jumped into her Jeep, and driven straight to Mr. Conroy's Los Angeles condominium. Now, facing his door in an interior hall of the luxury high-rise, Elizabeth wasn't so sure.

What if he's angry about last night? she worried, tugging on the edge of her white baby T-shirt in a vain attempt to make it cover her tan midriff. Despairing of ever making the T-shirt meet the waistband of her baggy sweatpants, Elizabeth decided to put on her windbreaker instead, zipping it all the way up to her chin. *He certainly can't accuse me of trying to seduce him,* she thought ironically, looking down at her shapeless outfit.

The elevator door behind her opened suddenly, and Elizabeth spun around, her pulse racing. What if it was him? A woman with a small child got out of the elevator, smiling pleasantly at Elizabeth before she walked down the hall and let herself into another condo.

I've got to get hold of myself, Elizabeth thought. *And if I'm ever going to do this, I have to do it now.* Summoning what courage she could, Elizabeth quickly raised her hand and rapped the heavy brass knocker.

Mr. Conroy answered almost immediately.

"Elizabeth! What a nice surprise," he exclaimed, smiling and looking genuinely pleased to see her.

At least he's not mad, she thought. "May I come in?" she asked.

"Of course! Please do." Mr. Conroy threw the lacquered white door open wide, motioning for Elizabeth to enter. "Can I take your jacket?" he offered.

"Uh . . . no," she stammered. "That's all right." She walked into the entryway of the condo, hugging the windbreaker to her sides. Slightly to her left was a formal dining room, and straight ahead was a sunken living room. The rooms were richly furnished and decorated, looking more like pictures in a magazine than anyplace someone might actually live. Plate-glass windows in both rooms dominated the back walls, opening onto the city below. The only hint that Mr. Conroy wasn't a bachelor living alone was the battered purple lunch box sitting incongruously on the dining-room table. Elizabeth wondered momentarily where Tom's young brother and sister were before she called herself back to the matter at hand.

"That's some view you have," she said.

"Do you like it?" Mr. Conroy asked eagerly. He hurried into the dining room and drew the vertical blinds to their limits so that Elizabeth could see the scene stretched out at their feet. "It'll be even prettier in an hour or so, when it gets dark and all the lights come on."

Elizabeth smiled weakly. *If I'm still here by then, I'll be in big trouble,* she thought.

"Can I get you anything? A soda?" Mr. Conroy offered.

"No. Thanks." She was surprised to hear her voice shaking. "Mr. Conroy . . . uh, George . . . we have to talk."

"Of course!" he agreed, looking way too pleased. Maybe she shouldn't have called him George. "Let's sit in the living room," he suggested.

Elizabeth let him lead her into the sunken living room, where he sat on a black leather sofa and motioned for her to sit beside him. Pretending not to see, she sat in a matching chair facing him instead.

"You don't want to sit there," he protested. "That chair's uncomfortable."

"I can't stay that long anyway," she said. "But we need to talk about last night."

Mr. Conroy looked somewhat abashed, but not repentant. "I rushed you," he said apologetically. "I should have waited for a better—"

"No," Elizabeth interrupted him. "You could have waited forever. What you did was totally off base."

"You . . . you don't think we could ever—"

"Never," she said firmly. "George, I'm in love with your son. Can't you see that?"

"Yes," he said slowly, all the happiness fading from his face. "I know. But—"

"But nothing. If Tom found out what you did,

it would break his heart. Is that what you want?"

Mr. Conroy dropped his head into his hands. "No. No, of course not," he said, his voice muffled.

"Is it worth throwing away a lifelong relationship with your son for a stupid mistake?" Elizabeth asked. It was nice seeing him squirm for a change instead of her.

"No. You're right," he said miserably, raising his head. "I've behaved like a total idiot. Can you ever forgive me?"

Elizabeth took a deep, happy breath. Nina was right after all—everything was going to work out fine.

"That's why I'm here," she told him honestly.

"I don't know what came over me. It's just . . . well . . . you make me feel so *alive*. For the first time since my wife . . ." His voice broke, and Elizabeth knew he'd been on the verge of reminding her that his wife had died a few years previously.

"I'm sorry about your wife," she said sympathetically. "And I'm hoping we can put all this behind us and go back to the way things were before."

Mr. Conroy nodded. "I'd like that. And I'm grateful to you, Elizabeth, for giving me a second chance. It won't happen again."

Elizabeth smiled. "I'm glad."

They sat there staring at each other from across the living room for a few moments, lost in their separate thoughts. Suddenly Elizabeth remembered the other thing she had to take care of.

"I want you to take this back," she said, fishing the gray jewelry box out of her pocket and placing it on the glass table between them. "I can't keep it."

"But you have to!" Mr. Conroy exclaimed, obviously distressed. "Don't you like it?"

"Of course I *like* it," she admitted, smiling. "But it's not right for me to accept such an expensive present from you."

"No!" Mr. Conroy insisted. "No, it's a thank-you gift—that's all. I'm perfectly comfortable telling Tom I gave it to you, and I know he'd want you to have it. Please keep it, Elizabeth."

Elizabeth hesitated, and Mr. Conroy took advantage of the pause to open the box and lift the locket up by its delicate gold chain. "My feelings will be hurt if you don't," he added, holding it out to her.

"George . . ." Elizabeth was more tempted than she would have thought possible before that moment. *Is there really any harm in taking his present, now that we have an understanding?* she wondered. Mr. Conroy could clearly afford to give her the necklace, and it *was* beautiful. Besides, he was insisting.

"Thank you," she said, reaching for the locket.

"Put it on," he urged.

Elizabeth complied shyly, clasping the chain behind her neck and settling the heart-shaped locket down over the front of her turquoise windbreaker. "I'm afraid my outfit doesn't do it justice," she joked, but even on nylon the diamonds were breathtaking.

"There'll be other outfits, and you'll look beautiful in them," Mr. Conroy said kindly, not at all in the suggestive way he'd complimented her in the restaurant. He was acting like his old self again, Elizabeth realized happily.

"Thanks. But I have to go now," she told him. "I have some studying to do for a couple of classes I missed today."

"Of course," Mr. Conroy said, rising to his feet. "I'm just so glad that you came by, Elizabeth. We'll see each other again soon."

"Yes. Soon," Elizabeth agreed, following him to the front door. Now that everything was cleared up between them, she'd be able to enjoy his company again. There'd be no reason that she and Tom couldn't include George in lots of the things they did. She reached the door and held out her hand to him. "Friends?" she asked, smiling.

"Friends," he agreed, taking her hand and shaking it. But when the handshake was over, he didn't let go. Instead, the same lovesick expression he'd worn the night before gradually took over his features.

"Mr. Conroy!" Elizabeth exclaimed, horrified, as she tried to yank her hand away. "Let go!"

"It's no use, Elizabeth. I love you!" He pulled her to him, trying desperately to kiss her.

"Stop it!" she cried, breaking free and fumbling for the doorknob. He was trying to slip his arms around her from behind when she wrestled open the door and struggled out of his grasp, stumbling into the elegant hall.

"How could you!" she accused him tearfully. "How could you do that?" She ran for the elevator, tears blurring her vision.

"Elizabeth, wait!" Mr. Conroy said, stepping out into the hall. "I'm so sorry. I'm weak!"

"You're pathetic!" she lashed out, backing up against the elevator doors. "I never want to see you again!"

The elevator opened, and Elizabeth stepped inside, her legs shaking. "And take this too!" she added, breaking the chain with the diamond locket off her throat and flinging it at him wildly.

"Don't go this way," Mr. Conroy begged as the necklace bounced harmlessly off his chest. "I'm weak, but I love you!"

The elevator doors started closing in the space between them.

"You're sick!" Elizabeth shouted through the narrowing crack. Mr. Conroy's love-struck face gradually disappeared from sight. Elizabeth sank to her knees on the carpeted floor of the luxurious elevator, sobbing as if her heart were breaking.

Chapter Ten

Jessica quickened her steps when Peterson Hall came into view, excited by the idea of catching Nick unawares. She'd never been to his dorm room before—for that matter, she'd never even been inside his building. *He'll be surprised to see me,* she congratulated herself, slipping through the lobby doors and joining a group of students waiting for an elevator. The elevator doors opened with a chime, and everybody piled in.

"Nine," Jessica said, flashing the guy standing closest to the floor buttons a brilliant smile. He pressed her button, along with everybody else's, and the elevator began its slow ascent.

Nick's floor was just one from the top, and Jessica had plenty of time to get totally excited as the elevator worked its way up, stopping at nearly every level. Nick hadn't invited her to come, so he wasn't expecting her—if she was lucky, she'd surprise him getting ready for tonight's secret meeting. Jessica checked her slender gold watch. It was nearly four-thirty. The elevator opened on the ninth floor, and she stepped confidently out into the hall. It might be a little early to catch Nick dressing up to play spy, but there had to be something she could learn from his room.

Walking down the dim, dirty hall, Jessica read the numbers on the doors. "Nine-eighteen," she said under her breath when she came upon Nick's. She took a moment to make sure her outfit was still OK—she was wearing white denim pants with a slinky silk blouse the exact blue-green color of her eyes—before she knocked on Nick's door.

"Who is it?" Nick called out in a sharp, tense voice.

Jessica raised her eyebrows at his tone. "Open up and see."

There was a long pause, accompanied by the sounds of shuffling, before the door finally opened. "Hi," Nick said, motioning for her to come inside. "I wasn't expecting you."

Jessica tossed her loose, freshly washed hair. "Then this is your lucky day," she said, breezing by him into his single dorm room. Jessica had heard the stories about how impossible singles were to get. Winston Egbert was the only other person she knew who had one, and that was a total mistake—Winnie also lived in an all-female dorm. Jessica's eyes roamed curiously about the room, hunting for clues to Nick's real identity. "So, how did you rate a single?" she asked.

Nick closed and locked the door, then took a seat on the bed. "Age before beauty," he said, grinning at her.

"Very funny," Jessica replied, but she took it as the compliment it was. She moved to Nick's tiny, narrow window and looked out over the campus. Even though they were nine floors up, there wasn't a lot to see—the lines of sight were mostly obstructed by other tall buildings. "Not much of a view," she observed.

"Not unless you find the roof of the library particularly attractive for some reason," Nick agreed.

Jessica giggled. "Liz would probably like it."

"Come, sit down," Nick urged, gesturing to the only chair in the room.

Jessica walked right past it and flopped onto the bed beside him instead. "Where's all your stuff?" she asked.

Nick's room was smaller than Jessica's bathroom at her parents' house, and there was far less inside it. The door was at one end, the window was at the other, and a single bed hugged the right wall. On the left wall was a built-in closet-desk-bookshelf combo and a desk chair. There was nothing on the desk or shelves, and the closet door was shut. The bed was covered with a plain, olive green spread, like a military bunk, and the walls were completely bare. Jessica turned to Nick, who was wearing old surplus green fatigues and a tight black T-shirt. "I feel like I'm in the army or something," she complained. How could she look for clues in an empty room?

Nick shrugged. "I'm not much of a decorator."

"To say the least! You don't have any pictures up or *anything.*" Most people Jessica knew at least had snapshots of their friends taped to the walls and usually a couple of posters too. "You're either really poor or really unimaginative," she concluded.

"I hope I'm not unimaginative," Nick told her, taking her into his arms and smiling suggestively just before he kissed her.

Jessica's arms went up around his neck and together they fell back against the ugly green bedspread, kissing passionately. *No, definitely not unimaginative.* She smiled to herself as the make-out session continued. As Nick's lips nibbled down her neck Jessica opened her eyes slightly to study the room again, but there was nothing there she hadn't already seen. *How can someone who lives like a monk kiss like the devil himself?* she wondered dreamily, closing her eyes again.

"So, what are you going to do tonight?" Nick asked at last.

Jessica smiled up at him. "You tell me."

Nick seemed to think about it as he pushed himself back into a sitting position and offered her a hand up too. "Well, I have to do some studying, but I should be done by about eight. Do you want to get together then?"

Liar, Jessica thought, smiling sweetly. "Why don't we study together?" she suggested. "I'll meet you in the library."

"The library? Uh, no." Nick didn't meet her eyes as he rose from the single bed. "I really prefer to study in my room."

"Then I'll go get my books and come back here."

"Jessica," Nick said, coming back to the bed. "You know I won't get anything done if you're here. You completely destroy my concentration."

Jessica laughed contentedly. Even if he was lying, at least he was flattering her while he did it. Still, she wasn't quite done with him. "But where are your books?" she asked, pointing to the empty shelves.

Nick looked almost shocked as he took in the bare bookshelves. "Oh . . . uh . . . in the closet," he stammered quickly. "I always keep them in there."

Jessica nodded and rose from the bed, stretching lazily. "How interesting."

"Yes, well, it's less messy," Nick explained.

Jessica could barely keep from laughing out loud at the unlikely thought of a mess in that sterile room. "So where should I meet you at eight?" she asked.

"I'll swing by your room," he said, the relief in his voice evident, "and we can go catch a late dinner somewhere."

"OK," she agreed, crossing to the door to leave.

"Oh . . . and Jessica?" Nick said as she reached it.

"Yes?"

"Don't change clothes."

Jessica smiled, knowing she looked terrific. "Don't worry," she said. Of course she had another outfit in mind for the seven o'clock pickup, but there'd be plenty of time to change back after that. "See you at eight," she added, closing Nick's door behind her. She walked to the elevator, turning her plan over in her mind.

If only he'd asked me to go with him to meet his contact tonight! Jessica thought, stepping into the empty elevator car and pushing the button marked G. *Then I wouldn't have to do what I'm about to do.*

Jessica reached the ground floor, then walked around to the back of the building and out into the residents' parking lot. Nick's black '67 Camaro was parked at the far edge, near some trees. Looking around to make sure no one was watching, Jessica popped the hood.

"Let's see," she muttered, leaning over the engine. "This ought to work." She reached out and loosened the coil wire, making sure that it still looked connected. *Thanks, Mike,* she thought as she put the hood back down and brushed off her hands. Being married to a mechanic had been an education in more ways than one.

Jessica was sure that Nick would be planning to drive to the meeting behind the science building, since it was all the way on the other side of campus. Unfortunately for Nick, his car wasn't going to start tonight. He could still walk to the meeting, of course, but by the time he realized he needed to, he'd already be late.

And just a little *late is all I need,* Jessica told herself excitedly, walking off across the parking lot in the direction of her dorm room. *Because I'll be right on time!*

Elizabeth put her head down on the desk of her favorite library carrel and covered it with her arms. It was dinnertime and the library was mostly empty, but she still didn't want anyone to hear her sobbing. She'd thought she'd cried herself dry in the Jeep on the way back to campus, but every time she remembered the way Mr. Conroy had betrayed her—betrayed *Tom*—Elizabeth started crying all over again. What was she going to do? Tom had never been happier in his life, and she was going to ruin everything for him.

She put a hand to her mouth, stifling the sounds of her unhappiness. She wished she could go to her room and have a good cry in private, but Elizabeth didn't want to face anyone—not even Jessica. Her hand moved from her mouth to the raised red welt on her neck, where the chain had cut her when she'd ripped off Mr. Conroy's necklace, and the sobs came faster. She'd believed in him—she'd even accepted his gift—and look how he'd repaid her!

"Liz? Are you OK?"

Elizabeth recognized Todd's concerned, familiar voice without looking up.

"I'm fine," she managed, pulling the turquoise windbreaker up over her head. She didn't want to see him, and she certainly didn't want him to see her in the state she was in. "Please, just leave me alone."

The scrape of a chair being pulled up beside her told Elizabeth that Todd had ignored her request. "What's the matter?" he asked gently, placing a comforting hand on her back. "I don't want to leave you like this."

Sobs overwhelmed Elizabeth again, and it was a long time before she could answer. Todd sat patiently at her side, rubbing her back lightly.

"Nothing's the matter," she said at last. How could she tell him, of all people, what was really wrong?

"I don't believe you," Todd said matter-of-factly. "Come on, Elizabeth, sit up and take that jacket off your head. Tell me what happened."

She didn't want to, but it was pretty clear he wasn't going away. Elizabeth did her best to wipe her face clean with her hands before she pulled the windbreaker back down to a normal position and sat up. She knew her looks must be wrecked from so much crying, and a quick, reluctant glance into Todd's eyes confirmed it.

"What happened to you!" he exclaimed, moving

to put an arm around her and pulling her tightly to his side. "Liz, are you sure you're all right?"

It felt surprisingly good to be back in Todd's arms—comfortable, safe.

She nodded against his SVU Basketball sweatshirt, breathing in his familiar smell. "I'm fine," she said. "I mean, I'm not hurt or anything."

"Then what happened?" he asked. "Please, Elizabeth, I want to help you."

To her total amazement, Elizabeth found herself blurting out the entire story. She was still dreading the thought of even mentioning it to Tom, yet suddenly she was spilling it all out for Todd, right down to the smallest detail. "I just don't know what to do!" she finished up miserably, wiping at her eyes. "The whole thing's such a mess." She pushed herself away from him and waited to hear what he'd say.

Todd sat silently in the chair beside her, obviously considering what she'd told him. For the first time that evening, Elizabeth took a good look at his face. *He's more handsome now than he's ever been,* she realized distractedly. But there was something else in his appearance too. He'd matured. He looked like a man.

"I think you have to tell Tom," Todd said at last.

"But I can't!" Elizabeth protested, snapping back to the subject. "Weren't you listening? It'll kill him!"

"Yes, I heard you," Todd said. "But don't you think he has a right to know? After all, he's a big boy. He doesn't need you to protect him from the truth."

"But he'll be so hurt!"

"Yes. Probably."

Elizabeth shook her head. "I can't do that to him."

"But Liz, don't you see? What Mr. Conroy did isn't your fault. It may hurt Tom, but you're not to blame."

"It sure feels like it," she said unhappily.

"You're not!" Todd took her hands in his and looked earnestly into her face. "Didn't you do everything you could to convince Mr. Conroy you weren't interested?"

Elizabeth couldn't speak as that afternoon's scene between her and Mr. Conroy pressed down on her recollection. She nodded instead, a tear slipping silently down her cheek.

Todd leaned forward and brushed the tear away. "You're going to have to tell him, Liz. Let Tom take care of it however he wants—it's not your problem anymore."

Todd actually made a lot of sense, Elizabeth realized with a sense of dawning relief. She *had* done everything she could think of to resolve the situation, and it was ultimately Tom's relationship with Mr. Conroy that was in question. Todd was right—she couldn't make a decision about something that important for Tom herself, yet that was in essence what she was doing by sheltering him from the truth. She'd have to tell him after all.

"I . . . I think you might be right," she said shakily.

Todd smiled encouragingly and squeezed her hands. "That's the spirit! Tom may be upset at first, but he'll thank you for it later."

"Do you think so?" she asked hopefully. It was hard to imagine being thanked for wrecking someone's world.

The single nod of Todd's head was emphatic. "I do."

"I guess I'll tell him, then."

"You should do it soon," Todd advised. "The longer you wait, the more it'll seem like you were trying to cover it up."

"I was only covering it up to save Tom's feelings!" Elizabeth protested.

"I know," Todd reassured her. "But it's just better to get it over with."

"Yes," Elizabeth agreed slowly. Todd was right. If she was really going to tell Tom, she should do it before he spent any more time with his father.

"Can I help at all?" Todd asked. "I mean, I know I can't do the hard part for you, but can I walk you over to Tom's dorm or something? You know, for moral support?"

Elizabeth smiled a little. *When did Todd become so sensitive?* she wondered. He really had grown up.

"Thanks," she said gratefully. "But you've already been a big help. I think I have to take care of things myself from here."

Todd reached forward and lifted a loose strand of hair from Elizabeth's face, smoothing it behind her ear. Then he straightened the front of her rumpled jacket, like a mother reluctant to send a child off on the first day of school. "OK," he said, "but just remember, I'm here if you need me."

Elizabeth nodded soundlessly. Todd was being so nice, she was getting choked up again. "Thanks," she managed at last.

Todd rose from his chair and stood by her carrel. Elizabeth's eyes rested on his long legs and the way his jeans came down over his high-tops before she lifted her head to say good-bye.

"See you soon," Todd said reassuringly. "And call me—anytime." Elizabeth's gaze followed him down the hall and out of her section of the library before her mind returned to the problem in front of her.

She'd tell Tom what his father had done, even though she knew it was going to devastate him. The thought of ruining Tom's happiness that way almost made Elizabeth change her mind again. *It would have been so much easier to spend the evening talking to Todd!* she thought longingly, turning her head to look in the direction he'd gone.

Jessica left Dickenson Hall with a last, furtive look around before she headed toward the science building. It was early—only six o'clock—but she wanted to be sure to meet Nick's contact *and* get there before Nick did. She wore the same spying outfit that she'd put together Saturday night—a long gray coat with a black turtleneck and leggings—but she'd replaced the felt hat with a flowing black scarf. The long, rectangular scarf covered her hair completely, then wrapped around her neck and trailed out behind her as she hurried along. It was a better disguise than the hat, and Jessica flattered herself that it set the proper mood of romantic danger too. Besides, she'd never much liked hats.

"Oh *no!*" Jessica exclaimed suddenly, stopping at the edge of the quad and smacking herself on the forehead. "The hat! Lila's going to *kill* me!" She looked at her watch, then stood rooted to the spot, unable to decide. She'd promised Lila a hundred times that she'd pick up that stupid hat, but how could she pass up this chance to find out about Nick? Still, Lila was counting on her.

"If I hurry, I can do both," Jessica said out loud, turning and running for the parking lot. Luckily she had the Jeep key in her coat pocket along with her room key, and she was pretty sure that her wallet was in the glove compartment. She ran at full speed, clearing the hedge at the edge of the parking lot like a hurdle and making a beeline for the bright red Jeep. *Thank goodness it's here,* she thought as she climbed into the driver's seat.

She'd wanted to use it to go shopping earlier, but Elizabeth had had it out somewhere.

Jessica started the engine with a roar and backed the Jeep out of its parking space, leaving tire rubber behind like a glaze on the blacktop. If she didn't hurry, Sweet Valley Milliners would close before she got there. Jessica pulled out into traffic in a panic as she headed for the mall. Unfortunately the first light at the corner turned red just as she got there, stopping her progress only a block from campus.

"Oh *no!*" Jessica groaned, slapping the dashboard in frustration. That was when she noticed that the gas gauge was on *E.* For the first time that Jessica could ever remember, Elizabeth had used all the gas and not refilled the tank.

"Elizabeth!" Jessica roared, ignoring the rarity of the offense and vowing to wreak grievous bodily harm on her twin as soon as she had the time. The light changed to green, and Jessica charged off the limit line, streaking down the street and into the full-service section of the college-area gas station. Jessica usually pumped her own gas, but since the self-serve pumps were all jammed with cars, full-serve would definitely be faster.

"Put in five bucks' worth!" she shouted at the uniformed guy who approached her before she turned her back on him to dig through the glove box for money. The tiny space was crammed with maps, receipts, sunglasses, and junk, and Jessica was relieved when she actually found her wallet. She pulled out a five-dollar bill and turned to pay the attendant.

"You want regular or super?" he asked, pointing to the pump.

"You haven't started yet?" Jessica screeched, leaping out of the Jeep and grabbing a nozzle herself. "I'm in a hurry here!"

The attendant removed the gasoline nozzle from her grip and leisurely inserted it into her gas tank. "You want me to clean your windows?" he asked while dripping in the gasoline one slow ounce at a time.

"No! I *want* to get out of here." Jessica jumped back into the driver's seat and slammed the door to emphasize her point.

The attendant smiled what he obviously believed was a devastatingly handsome smile. "What's your hurry?" he asked, winking.

It was unbelievable—she was in the biggest hurry of her life, and this idiot was trying to *flirt* with her! Jessica looked at the pump and saw that it had barely passed the three-dollar mark.

"Hand me my gas cap," she ordered, holding her hand out the window to him.

"What—" he began.

"Give it to me!" she shouted.

Moving as if he were underwater, the attendant reached the cap off the top of the pump and slowly extended it toward Jessica. She snatched it, throwing the five-dollar bill at him with her other hand. "Keep the change," she said, peeling out of the parking lot and leaving him pumping gas into empty air.

Jessica cursed the slow-moving loser at the gas station all the way to the shopping center, but at last she pulled into the enormous mall parking lot and parked as close as she could to the hat store. It was getting late and the lot was almost deserted. Jessica knew she had to hurry. Leaping from the Jeep, she ran into the mall through a side entrance, flying down the polished stone floor at a dead run. She reached Sweet Valley Milliners just as the owner was locking the door.

"No! Please!" Jessica begged, glancing at her watch. It was six-thirty—closing time. "I have to pick up a hat for Lila Fowler. It's important!"

"Oh! Come on in, then," the woman shopkeeper said kindly, opening up again and motioning Jessica inside.

"Thanks a million," Jessica gushed as she bustled into the store and hurried toward the service counter. "Lila would have killed me if I'd missed you." An ugly thought struck Jessica at the sight of the cash register. Lila's taste was notoriously expensive—this hat was probably going to cost more than Jessica's parents gave her to live on for an entire month. "You *can* put this on Lila's account, right?" she asked.

"Don't worry about that," the woman said,

walking around behind the register. "It's already been paid for." She reached under the counter and produced an enormous, pink-flowered hatbox.

"How big is this hat!" Jessica exclaimed, shocked. She couldn't go meet Nick's contact carrying a box like that, but if she left it in the Jeep, someone would steal it for sure.

"Would you like to see it?" the shopkeeper asked happily, misunderstanding Jessica completely. Before Jessica could stop her, the kindly older woman had removed the lid from the box, holding the hat up for Jessica's inspection. "I think this is one of the prettiest hats we've ever done," she said proudly, turning it so that Jessica could admire it from every angle.

"It's very nice," Jessica replied tersely, looking repeatedly from the hat to the box and praying the woman would get the message.

"This fabric came all the way from London," the hatmaker said, brushing her hand lovingly along the shimmering white width of the large, floppy brim. "And see this lace?" The woman pointed to the shallow crown of the hat, which was overlain with rich-looking white lace. "French," she said, dropping her voice confidentially. "Your friend has good taste."

"The best. Now I've really got to—"

"When she first ordered it," the shopkeeper interrupted, "I wasn't sure if I was going to like it. I was afraid the lace might get lost in a white-on-white combination. I thought perhaps pink . . ."

Jessica wanted to scream with impatience as the woman droned on and on about the exciting history of Lila's stupid hat. In another second Jessica was going to know where the *thread* had come from. Or if she was really lucky, she'd find out who'd had the exciting job of manufacturing the label that proclaimed the hat to be a Sweet Valley Milliners Original. "Excuse me, but I have to go," Jessica blurted suddenly.

The shopkeeper looked taken aback, then seemed to realize that Jessica had only been rude out of desperation. "I'm sorry, dear," she said apologetically, placing the hat back into the box. "I should have noticed you were in a hurry."

A few more precious moments passed before the box was closed to the shopkeeper's satisfaction and the pink string carrying handles were attached. When the hat was finally handed over, it was all Jessica could do to stop herself from tearing it out of the woman's hands.

"Thanks," she said, already running for the door. "I really do appreciate this." Whatever the shopkeeper might have said in return was lost as Jessica sped out of the store, the big round hatbox clasped to her chest to allow maximum running speed.

Jessica crashed through the doors leading outside to the parking lot, then threw the hatbox into the passenger side of the Jeep. It was six-forty-five. *Hurry, hurry, hurry,* she chanted to herself as she climbed in on the driver's side and tore out of the parking lot. She could still make it—if everything went *perfectly.* She'd drive straight to the parking lot nearest the science building, she decided, turning the wheel sharply and careening down a side street. That way she could get there faster.

After ten minutes that seemed like an eternity, Jessica finally drove into the science lot and parked. The sun had gone down while she'd been chasing around after Lila's hat, and it was already dark in the parking lot. Jessica knew it would be even darker behind the science building, and she felt a familiar thrill of excitement at the thought of meeting Nick's contact. She hesitated just a moment to check her reflection in the rearview mirror, adjusting her scarf and dark glasses. She was ready.

Jessica hurried up the stairs from the parking lot, her heart beating time to the rhythm of the hatbox bouncing off her knees. *I can't believe I'm stuck carrying this stupid thing,* she thought, throwing a disgusted glance at the garish box. Even though it probably didn't matter, Jessica still couldn't help regretting the way it ruined her entire look. It was worse than the time her mother had sent her to school with a Barbie backpack.

Oh, well, she consoled herself, *if everything goes according to plan, I'll be in and out before Nick even sees me.*

Chapter Eleven

"Now, sugar," Celine said nervously, looking Jordan over. He stood just inside her front door. "Are you sure you know what to do?"

"I already told you—I'm ready, Celine."

He doesn't look *ready,* Celine observed as she took in Jordan's anxious expression and pathetic excuse for an inconspicuous outfit. He was wearing that ridiculously large baseball cap and an SVU Engineering sweatshirt with jeans. *Why not just pin a note to his shirt that says "Hi, I'm Jordan Wilson?"* Celine asked herself sarcastically, trying to decide if she should make him go home and change clothes. She checked her watch—no time.

"Well, now, Jordan, I know you're ready. I just want to make sure you understand what's going to happen."

Jordan looked at her, a little hostilely, she thought. "What's to understand, Celine? I meet a guy named Nick behind the science building and I hand him some papers. Period."

It took every ounce of self-control she had to keep from strangling him on the spot. "No, sugar," she said calmly. "Aren't you forgetting something?"

Jordan seemed to consider. "No. I don't think so."

"The *return* packet!" Celine reminded him. "Don't forget to make Nick give you the return packet!"

"Oh yeah," Jordan said slowly, his pale eyes clouding. "What's in that package I'm supposed to pick up again?"

"I already told you," Celine said, struggling to keep the irritation from her voice. If Jordan kept on stalling this way, he was going to be late to meet Nick. "It's just more papers."

"But Celine. I still don't understand why *Nick's* giving *us* papers. I mean, what are we going to do with—"

"You don't have to understand!" Celine exploded, losing her patience at last. "Just do it!"

Jordan stepped back, a wounded expression on his pale features. "I just think—"

"Don't think!"

He pulled his baseball cap down lower over his forehead, averting his eyes from hers. "I don't have to do this, you know," he said sulkily.

Celine checked her watch again. It was two minutes to seven, and her apartment was at least a five-minute walk from the meeting place. If Jordan didn't show up on time, Nick might get spooked and leave. She didn't have a minute to fool around.

"Oh, baby. I'm sorry," she said, stepping forward and twining her arms around his skinny neck. "I'm just so worried about my poor brother. You can understand that, can't you?"

"I don't know," Jordan said, still sulky.

"I'd explain things better if I could, but sometimes you just have to trust people." She kissed him then, tugging gently at his bottom lip as she pulled away. "You *do* trust me, don't you, Jordan?"

"I guess."

"You guess?" She kissed him again, putting everything she had into it. By the time she'd finished, she practically had to hold him up to keep him from falling. "How about now?"

"I trust you," he said.

Celine smiled. "That's better. You'd should get going, then, sugar. You're going to be late."

"OK," Jordan agreed, reluctantly letting her go. "Let's get this over with."

Celine walked from near the front door, where she'd been standing with Jordan, into the kitchen. Opening the cabinet under the sink, she reached all the way to the back and pulled out the package.

"Here are the papers," she said, crossing the living room again and handing the bundle to Jordan. "Remember—don't give them to anyone but Nick."

Jordan took the package from her, examining it curiously, and Celine breathed a mental sigh of relief that she'd taken the time to disguise it. She'd put the small package the men on the boat had given her into a larger box that had once held letter-size sheets of writing paper. After stuffing crumpled-up newspaper into all the spaces between the original package and the new, bigger box, Celine had taped the outside of the box closed and wrapped the entire thing in plain brown paper from an old grocery bag, using most of a roll of tape on the outside just to make sure no one peeked. The result was a brown, paper-wrapped parcel the size of a major stack of documents.

"OK," Jordan said, tucking the package under his arm. "I'll come back here when it's over."

"No!" Celine panicked. The last thing she needed was for this nitwit to inadvertently lead someone back to her apartment. "I mean, we should celebrate," she improvised, her voice back under control. "Meet me at that cute little coffeehouse off campus, and we'll go somewhere from there."

Not that she had any intention of actually showing up, of course—that would be too dangerous. No, she'd sneak over to his dorm room later with some story about how she'd missed him at the Java Joint. Then she'd pick up her money and it would be bye-bye, Jordan.

Jordan nodded and opened the door. "See you in a little while, then," he said before he headed down the hall. He was all the way out of sight before Celine thought of something that totally rocked her.

What if Nick didn't come in person? After all, *she* was sending a patsy—why shouldn't he? What if he sent someone else and Jordan was too stupid to figure it out?

Not that it would be entirely his fault, Celine had to admit to herself as she began to run. She'd probably told Jordan a hundred times not to give the package to anyone but Nick. Celine reached the end of the hall and practically flung herself into the stairwell, taking the chipped concrete stairs two at a time in spite of her high heels and tight skirt. "Jordan!" she shouted, clearing the building. "Jordan, wait up!"

She caught him at the edge of the parking lot.

"What's the matter?" he asked, puzzled.

"I just thought of something," Celine panted, trying to catch her breath. She had the awful feeling that every window in the apartment building was watching them like an eye, but there was nothing she could do about it now. "Nick might not come in person," she explained. "He might send someone else."

Jordan's face immediately took on the same anxious expression she'd kissed off only minutes before. "Why would he do that?" he asked.

"I don't know, Jordan," Celine improvised. "Nick's a busy guy. It will probably be him, but don't count on it, OK? You'll just have to keep your eyes open and use your head a little."

Jordan looked injured. "I'm perfectly capable of thinking for myself, Celine," he said, turning his back on her and walking off in the direction of the science building.

Yeah, right, she thought. But she couldn't very well tell Jordan that she'd chosen him for this job precisely because she was sure that he wasn't.

It won't be the end of the world if Jordan messes up tonight and doesn't get the package delivered, Celine reassured herself nervously, watching his retreating back. If she had to, she could set up the delivery again for tomorrow. But that would take time. And time was the one thing Celine was running out of.

Jessica waited behind the science building, her heart racing with exertion, excitement, and just a tinge of fear. It was quite dark, but even so she felt extremely conspicuous holding Lila's brightly flowered hatbox. *Just play it cool,* she told herself firmly, trying to strike a casual pose. It was hopeless, she realized after a few seconds. She looked like a dork.

Switching the hatbox into her right hand, Jessica checked her watch again. It was almost 7:10—Nick's contact was late. If he didn't show up soon, there was a chance that Nick would get there before Jessica had had a chance to intercept the guy and find out what was in those documents. *Hurry up!* she prayed silently, peering down the overgrown path into the darkness.

Then a horrible thought occurred to her. What if the contact had called Nick again since she'd overheard them the day before? What if they'd changed the meeting place or the time? She could be standing there for absolutely no reason while the entire exchange was taking place somewhere else.

"No," she whispered under her breath. "It has to be here!" If she didn't find out Nick's true story soon, she'd go crazy.

A minute later Jessica heard footsteps crunching in the gravel behind her. She whirled to see who was coming and found herself face-to-face with a young-looking guy wearing jeans and a sweatshirt, a baseball cap that looked too big for him pulled down low on his head. *He's not old enough to be a spy,* she thought, disappointed. *He looks more like a lost Little Leaguer.* He must be a student, Jessica decided, eyeing the SVU Engineering logo on his sweatshirt. She moved to the edge of the path without a word, planning to let him walk by.

"Um . . . miss?" the young guy said tentatively. "Were you waiting for a package?"

A totally unexpected thrill raced through her as Jessica realized that the guy was Nick's contact after all. She'd pulled it off!

"Yes," she said, holding out her hand. "Do you have it?"

The guy hesitated for a second, then extended a paper-wrapped parcel the size of a large textbook. Jessica tried to curb her excitement and nervousness as she took the package from him. The unusually long brim of the contact's baseball cap sheltered his face, and Jessica couldn't see him well under the shadow it created. Even so she got the distinct impression that he was tense, edgy—maybe even dangerous.

"Very good," she said airily, trying to disguise her fear. "I'll make sure the consulate gets these documents." She tucked the package under her arm and waited to see what would happen next.

Nick's contact looked up at her for a second, seemingly confused, then ducked his head, hiding his face again. "Aren't you supposed to give me something too?" he whispered hoarsely.

Was she? Jessica racked her brain, trying to think. *Of course!* He expected to be paid for his documents, just like the guy she'd met before. A cold sensation of fear coursed through her as Jessica remembered how angry the other contact had become when he'd discovered she had no money. *How could I have made the same stupid mistake twice?* she asked herself frantically. Her breathing quickened—she had to think. Who knew what this guy would do if she stiffed him? He might even kill her! But Jessica didn't have any money. In fact, the only thing she could possibly give him was . . .

"Here," she said abruptly, extending Lila's hatbox. "I think you'll find everything in here."

The contact nodded, taking the hatbox awkwardly by its pink string handles. A split second later he was sprinting down the path at a dead run.

Oh, man, Jessica groaned to herself as his thin form receded into the night, *Lila's going to be furious!* The thought of her best friend's certain displeasure temporarily marred Jessica's big triumph, but it took only a few seconds for Jessica to put things back in perspective. If Lila was truly her best friend, then of course she'd want to do her part to help solve this mystery. *And after all,* Jessica told herself, looking down at the bundle she now held in both hands, *I got the package. I just know this is the key to all Nick's secrets!* Jessica smiled with satisfaction as she made her way back down the pathway toward the stairs and from there down to the parking lot.

The science lot was deserted except for her Jeep and one or two other cars parked around the edges. As she walked toward the Jeep, Jessica congratulated herself on the fact that she'd driven to the meeting. Even though she hadn't originally planned to, now she'd be able to get back to her room that much faster to open Nick's package and see what it contained. She knew it was documents, of course—she'd learned that much by eavesdropping on Nick's phone conversation—but what *type* of documents would they be? There were so many different, exciting possibilities.

Jessica turned the package over in her hands as she walked, feeling its weight. It didn't look like much—especially not after all the effort she'd expended to get it. The tightly taped brown paper that covered it was completely without markings to reveal its contents. "What little secrets do you hold?" she asked it in a playful whisper.

Suddenly a dazzling light ripped through the darkened parking lot, blinding her. "Freeze!" thundered a voice from somewhere nearby.

Jessica faltered, terrified. She couldn't see, but she could hear running footsteps closing in from all sides. "What . . . ?" she tried to ask, turning toward the voice.

"I said freeze! Don't move or I'll shoot!"

Elizabeth paused outside the SVU television station offices, gathering her courage. Half of her was hoping to find Tom alone inside and the other half was hoping not to find him at all. She'd already been to his dorm room, where his roommate, Danny Wyatt, had told her to try the station. Elizabeth took a deep breath and fidgeted with the buttons on her new pink sweater. One thing was sure—if she didn't find Tom soon, she was going to lose her nerve.

The door opened suddenly, making Elizabeth jump.

"Hey, Elizabeth. What are you doing here so late?" Brad Jefferson, one of the new WSVU interns, was leaving the station.

"Looking for Tom," she answered, keeping her voice light. "Have you seen him lately?"

Brad jerked a thumb back in the direction of the door. "Yeah, he's in there. I don't know what he's doing, though. He's going through tape archives dating back to the dawn of television."

"Probably just to the dawn of his freshman year," Elizabeth guessed, doing her best to smile. "Thanks, Brad."

"No problem." Brad took off down the hallway, and Elizabeth pushed through the door into the station.

The irony of the situation wasn't lost on Elizabeth as she walked slowly toward the archive room, trying to plan what to say. Tom was looking for more of his old news stories to show Mr. Conroy, of course. Elizabeth was sure of it. How was she ever going to tell Tom that this new father he idolized wasn't who he appeared to be?

Elizabeth stuck her head through the doorway into Tape Storage. Tom was sitting alone in a cloud of dust, old cardboard boxes full of videotapes strewn around the floor beside him.

"Hi, Liz!" he called excitedly when he saw her. "I didn't expect to see you today. Jessica said you were sick."

"I feel better . . . ," Elizabeth started to lie, but

Tom talked right over the end of her sentence without listening.

"I was just pulling out a couple more stories to show George. There's some really great stuff in here."

Elizabeth smiled weakly. Tom didn't notice.

"I've got the athletics scandal series and most of the other stories we did together too," he said, "but I can't decide what to give him from my early pieces. What do you think—'Teenage Gambling' or 'The Evils of Tenure'?"

"Yeah," Elizabeth said distractedly, pulling up a folding chair. "Sounds good."

Tom finally looked at her, the videotapes in both hands temporarily forgotten. "It wasn't a yes-or-no question."

"What? Oh . . . 'Teenage Gambling,' I guess."

"Do you think so?" he asked excitedly. "I always thought that was a good piece too, but the tenure story got more attention."

Elizabeth shrugged. "I never saw either one," she reminded him, her voice coming out short and annoyed in spite of her good intentions.

Tom looked at her in shock for a moment before her words finally seemed to sink in. He dropped the tapes into the closest box, stood up, and pulled a folding chair up beside her. "I guess I *have* been a little into myself the last few days," he said apologetically. "I'm sorry."

Elizabeth closed her eyes, willing the tears she

felt to stay trapped behind her lids. When she opened them again, Tom was staring at her with genuine concern. He wasn't making what she had to do any easier.

"I need to talk to you about your father," she said, taking a deep, shaky breath.

"He's great, isn't he?" Tom enthused. "I still can't believe it. I know I've said this before, Elizabeth, but I'll never be able to thank you for—"

"No!" she interrupted, her voice echoing in the tiny room. She couldn't bear his gratitude—not now. "Please don't thank me," she added more quietly.

"But Liz . . . ," he began, confused.

She turned to face him, the tears she'd been trying to hold back spilling over at last. "Tom, I'm so sorry, but we've got a problem."

"What?" His dark eyes searched hers worriedly. "What's the matter?"

"It's about your dad."

Tom's expression froze. "Did something happen to him? He's hurt, isn't he?" Tom's voice was loud with panic, and he was halfway out of his chair before Elizabeth could grab his sleeve and pull him back down.

"Nothing like that," she said.

"What, then? Tell me!"

"Tom, you know how much I liked your father. But I've known him longer than you have—maybe in some ways I know him better."

Tom opened his mouth to respond, but Elizabeth rushed ahead. "He's been making passes at me, Tom. It started at Andre's, when you were in the bathroom. I tried to convince myself that I'd misunderstood, but then after the concert last night—when you went to get the tapes—he grabbed me and tried to kiss me."

"Kiss you," Tom repeated. His eyes were unreadable.

"I know," Elizabeth said. "I was as shocked as you are. But there was no way I could doubt his intentions after that. I didn't want to have to tell you, Tom—I didn't want to hurt you. But your dad is a very sick man."

"Do you think so?" Tom asked weakly. He wasn't looking at her anymore.

Elizabeth put her hands over one of his, where it rested on his knee. "I'm so sorry. But yes, I do. I went to his condo this afternoon to tell him to leave me alone. I thought that if he and I could get things straight between us . . ." Elizabeth's throat closed with emotion at the too recent memory of how Mr. Conroy had treated her. "Anyway," she managed, "it didn't work."

Tom was silent for a minute, his head turned away from her. Elizabeth could barely stand to imagine the hurt he must be feeling. *At least it's out in the open now,* she comforted herself, squeezing his unresponsive hand. *We can work through this together.* At last Tom turned to face her.

"I can't believe you're that jealous," he said. His eyes were hard, closed off.

"What?" she gasped.

"I see what you're doing, Elizabeth," he said coldly. "Don't think I don't. You can't stand to share the attention, can you?"

"That's not true!" Elizabeth protested. Never in her wildest dreams had it occurred to her that Tom would turn against her over this. "Your father has a problem, Tom. Two different times he grabbed me against my will and tried—"

"Oh yes," Tom interrupted sarcastically, "tried to kiss you. I'm sorry, Liz, but that's the stupidest thing I've ever heard. You're just not that irresistible."

Elizabeth stared at him in shock. It was the meanest thing he'd ever said to her.

"You know what I think?" Tom went on. "I don't think you *want* me to be happy. The last few years of my life have been hell—total hell. And now, when I finally find a little happiness, you want to ruin it."

"I do not!" Elizabeth cut in.

"It sure looks that way to me. I have a family again—I'm happy—but you're so jealous of the time my father is taking away from our relationship that you stoop to these pathetic lies. I never knew you were so selfish, Liz."

Elizabeth stood up, trembling all over. The emotions running through her were so strong and confused that she barely knew what to say. She was sorry for hurting Tom, but now he'd hurt her too. And insulted her. And refused to listen. Her tears still fell, but they were no longer tears of sympathy—now they were the bitter tears of anger, frustration, and hurt pride.

"How dare you accuse me of lying?" she demanded hysterically. "Or say that you've never been happy? How lucky for you that Mr. Conroy came along to save you from the *hell* of being with me."

"Yeah, that's right!" Tom fired back, rising to face her. "Wake up, Liz. I don't need you anymore. And if this is how you're going to act, I don't even *want* you."

Her hand shot out so quickly that Elizabeth didn't know she was going to slap him until she felt the sharp sting in her palm and saw the red marks of her fingers outlined on Tom's white cheek. Then the sudden realization of the unforgivable thing she'd done was as sobering as an ice-cold shower.

"Tom," she gasped, horrified. "I'm so sorry. I . . . I didn't mean it."

"Just get out," he said, turning his back on her.

"Tom . . ." She tried to put her arms around him from behind and press her wet, miserable face against the comforting softness of his flannel shirt, but he held himself apart from her—stiff, rigid.

"Get out," he said again. His voice was dead to her, as if they'd never even known each other.

Elizabeth tried one more time. "Tom, I—"

"Out!" he shouted angrily, twisting from her grasp. "Get away from me!"

Elizabeth hesitated for a moment, straining unsuccessfully to hear any trace of love in his voice. Then she ran sobbing from the room, from the station building, and out into the night. Her hands covered her face as she fled blindly, running in no particular direction. She just knew she had to get away.

Away from what? she asked herself bitterly, still feeling the sting in her rebellious right hand. *Tom or myself?* The tears overcame her then, and she ran up onto some deserted grass off the edge of the quad, throwing herself down on her stomach to cry. She was going to get a cold, maybe catch pneumonia, but she didn't care. All she cared about was Tom.

How could I have been so insensitive? Elizabeth berated herself miserably. *I knew he was happy—I shouldn't have interfered with that.* For a moment it occurred to her that she'd done the best she could to spare Tom pain, whereas his attack on her had been totally unfounded. Elizabeth felt another brief flush of anger as she recalled the heartless things Tom had said to her, but then she remembered the violent way she'd responded and was overwhelmed by shame instead.

I'm never going to see him again, she thought. Suddenly all the little hairs stood up on the back of Elizabeth's neck, as if she'd experienced a premonition. *No!* she thought desperately. *That can't be true.* The very idea made her weak. It wasn't possible. Was it?

Was her relationship with Tom over for good?

"Oh, man." Noah groaned, rubbing his stomach gingerly. "I feel like I swallowed a bowling ball."

Alex giggled. "You say the same thing every time you eat the cafeteria meat loaf. When are you going to learn?"

"It always *sounds* like a good idea," Noah defended himself. "Is it my fault our cafeteria could mess up hot water?"

Alex smiled and took her boyfriend's hand as they walked across campus on their way to the library. "Next time try something else," she suggested.

It was great to be back with Noah. Even listening to him complain about the food in the cafeteria seemed wonderful compared to being without him. Alex walked beside him happily, feeling as if her life was starting to take a turn for the better. Not only had she and Noah made up, but in only three days she'd helped make a real difference at the substance abuse hot line. It was the most incredible feeling, being there for someone who really needed her.

"How are things going at the hot line?" Noah asked, startling her.

"What, are you a mind reader now?" Alex exclaimed.

Noah laughed. "Lucky guess."

"It's going really well," Alex said proudly, returning to his question. "I definitely know why you did it."

"It can be a real rush," Noah agreed. "But every now and then it can drive you crazy too."

"What do you mean?"

"You know. Sometimes you get a caller who you just can't help, and you feel like you ought to do *something,* but there's nothing you can do."

Alex was silent, remembering the strange call she'd taken that morning from the guy who thought his girlfriend was involving him in a drug deal.

"I guess that hasn't happened to you yet," Noah added.

"What? Oh, uh, no. Not really." How could she tell him . . . the calls were confidential.

"Well, it will," Noah said sagely. "And when it does, just try not to let it keep you up worrying all night. I used to get calls from this one girl named Enid that almost drove me right out of my mind."

"Very funny!" Alex laughed, smacking him playfully on the arm. They had reached the library and were starting up the stairs when Noah stopped, his attention focused on something in the quad.

"Did you see that weirdo?" he asked, hesitating outside the library door and smiling in disbelief.

Alex turned her head to look in the direction of Noah's gaze. The quad outside the library was dimly lit by yellow lights at intervals around the edge of the concrete, but Alex couldn't see anything there except a few reasonably normal-looking students going about their business.

"No," she said. "Where?"

"Some dude just ran by carrying this huge pink hatbox." Noah shook his head, as if he pitied the runner. "Poor guy is probably in the middle of some humiliating frat prank."

"That's the big contact?" said an incredulous voice at Jessica's back. "It's just a girl!"

"Can't judge a book, I guess," another man's voice replied. "Get up," he ordered Jessica.

Jessica tried to push herself up off the asphalt of the parking lot, but her shaking legs wouldn't obey her. The best she could do was hands and knees. After their lights had blinded her, the two men had forced her to the ground, frisked her for weapons, and taken her package. She was still so scared, she thought she might throw up.

"On your feet, I said!" The second officer grabbed her by the back of her overcoat and jerked her into a standing position. "Let's go."

"Go where?" Jessica asked. The men seemed to ignore her.

"Hey, Luke!" the first one called loudly across the parking lot. "Come take a look at our kingpin!"

Jessica lifted her head to see a group of uniformed policemen surrounding four squad cars that had screeched in while she'd been on the ground. The second officer laughed at his partner's humor and began pushing Jessica roughly in the direction of the squad cars. The cars' revolving lights illuminated the parking lot in rhythmic flashes, adding bursts of colored brilliance to the white floodlight. The entire scene was surreal.

"But what did I do?" Jessica protested weakly as they reached the cars.

"If I were you, I wouldn't talk," the first officer advised her, not unkindly. Jessica felt a flicker of hope before the second officer pushed her face-down onto the hood of one of the vehicles.

"Don't move," he ordered, taking a step backward with her package. Jessica could sense rather than see the other officers crowding around as the one with the package examined it just outside her line of sight. She heard the wrapping paper rip, then there was a pause followed by the sound of more ripping paper.

"Five hundred grams of cocaine!" the policeman announced triumphantly.

"Cocaine!" Jessica screeched. What was he talking about?

Before they could stop her, Jessica pushed herself off the hood of the squad car and spun to face the officers. Her scarf disguise was already half off her head, but she still wore the dark glasses. Jessica whipped them off in a panic so that the policemen could see the honesty in her eyes. "There's some kind of mistake!" she told them, squinting into the light.

"Jessica!" she heard a familiar voice gasp.

"Nick! Thank goodness!" Jessica had no idea what Nick was doing there, standing beside the cop who had taken her package, but the flood of relief she experienced at the sight of him was overwhelming. Everything would be all right now. Jessica would tell Nick what had happened, and he'd convince the policemen of her innocence.

"Nick, this is a big mix-up!" she cried. "I can explain!"

A few of the officers laughed. "They can *all* explain," Jessica heard one say.

Nick looked at her sadly, his expression tortured.

Why wasn't he doing anything? What was the matter? "Nick, *say* something!" Jessica begged, reaching out her arms to him.

Nick's face twisted with pain, then closed off completely. He stepped forward quickly and closed cold metal handcuffs over her outstretched wrists.

"Nick! What's—"

Nick shook his head, cutting her off. "You have the right to remain silent . . . ," he began.

***Is this the end for Nick and Jessica? Can Nick actually send Jessica to jail? Find out in Sweet Valley University #26,* THE TRIAL OF JESSICA WAKEFIELD.**